This book belongs to:

welcome
BOOKS

New York • San Francisco

Edited by **Katrina Fried**
& Lena Tabori

Design by **Jon Glick**

THE **LITTLE BIG**
BOOK FOR

BRIDES

TABLE OF CONTENTS

TRADITIONS & LORE

READINGS & POETRY

SEVEN YEARS AGO, on a soggy Saturday in May, I walked down the aisle towards the beaming and teary-eyed face of my husband, Matt. I can still recall without effort the growing feelings of elation, spirit, and overwhelming emotion with each step I took closer to my beautiful groom and our future together. Ours was an intimate ceremony and celebration, attended by close family and friends. Their love and support created

My Best Day

such a joyful energy, I thought we might just raise the roof of our little one-room chapel. It was, and still is, my very best day.

A celebration and reminder of the meaning of marriage, *The Little Big Book for Brides* is the book I wish I had on my bedside table when I was a bride-to-be. I hope it will be a treasured possession for you in the months to come. Curl up for a read anytime you want to relax and rejuvenate or seek entertainment and inspiration. There are wonderful stories and essays about being a bride and becoming a wife; beautiful poems, readings, and quotes on the topics of love and marriage; interesting traditions and superstitions about courtship, engagement, and weddings; great activities and crafts to do throughout your engagement; even delicious recipes for some of the festivities that often precede and follow a wedding.

My favorite category in this volume is Advice. The excerpts come from a variety of sources, including a judge, a father, a psychologist, and a spiritualist, to name a few. Some are filled with humor, others are poignant and touching, all are honest and, in my experience, true. And then there's the advice my mother gave me on my wedding day: Come from love, speak the truth, act with integrity, and you'll never go wrong. It's the best advice I ever got.

Katrina Fried
Editor

We two form a multitude.

OVID

ADVICE: *Advice For a Happy Marriage*

Written by Miss Dietz's third-grade class as a wedding gift to their teacher.

YOU NEED TO KISS EVERY ONCE IN A WHILE.

I THINK YOU SHOULD WEAR SOMETHING BEAUTIFUL.

GET BUNNIES.

TAKE TURNS DOING THE CHORES.

WHEN YOUR HUSBAND'S GRUMPY, GIVE HIM SOME COFFEE.

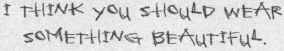

TO SHOW YOU LOVE EACH OTHER,
TAKE THE SMALLEST COOKIE.

MOSTLY SAY YES. (LIKE IF YOU'RE GOING TO
HAVE HOT DOGS FOR DINNER
AND YOU REALLY DON'T
LIKE HOT DOGS, IT'S
OKAY TO SAY NO.)

TAKE BREAKS FROM
EACH OTHER
ONCE IN A WHILE.

SLEEP TOGETHER.

DO NOT MARRY
ANOTHER PERSON.

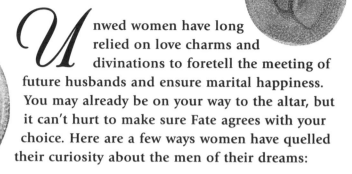

*U*nwed women have long relied on love charms and divinations to foretell the meeting of future husbands and ensure marital happiness. You may already be on your way to the altar, but it can't hurt to make sure Fate agrees with your choice. Here are a few ways women have quelled their curiosity about the men of their dreams:

He loves me, he loves me not...

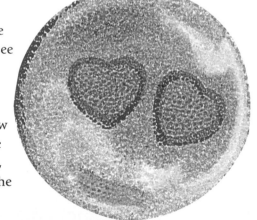

❧ ON CHRISTMAS EVE, stand before the fireplace and gaze into the flames to see the image of your future husband.

❧ IF YOU LOVE A MAN and want to know if he will propose, throw a nut into the fire and say his name. If the nut jumps, you'll marry. If the nut doesn't move, the relationship will have no spark.

❦ IN CASE YOU ARE LUCKY enough to be a bridesmaid, plant a sprig of myrtle in front of the newlyweds' home. If it takes root, you'll marry within the year.

❦ YOU CAN LEARN the temperament of your future husband by plucking a piece of hay from a hayloft at midnight. A crooked piece foretells a surly man; a straight piece signifies a good-natured mate.

✿ PEEL AN APPLE in a single strip and toss the peel over your left shoulder. The shape of the peel will reveal the first letter of the name of your spouse to be.

❦ OR PLUCK SOME WILD DAISIES from a nearby field and put the roots under your pillow to dream of your groom.

❦ ON ALL HALLOWS EVE, brush your hair three times in front of a mirror. If you glimpse a man standing behind you, wedding bells will ring before the year is through.

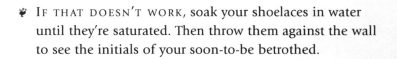

❦ WHEN ATTENDING A WEDDING, be sure to take a piece of groom's cake home and put it under your pillow. That night the face of your future husband will appear in your dreams.

❦ IF THAT DOESN'T WORK, soak your shoelaces in water until they're saturated. Then throw them against the wall to see the initials of your soon-to-be betrothed.

Dear Meg,

I just got back from our walk together and our good discussion (or call it loving argument) about your plans. Although I was honest, I haven't said all I want to say. I want to talk to you about life, love, and an enduring relationship with a man.

Your choice will be the most personal, intimate, and significant life choice you'll make. I want you to benefit from my mistakes and from my learnings.

First the learnings. When I chose your father, there were rational factors in my decision.

CHOOSING YOUR LOVE

FROM FROM THE HEART

Call it reason, call it love, it doesn't matter. But these things were certain. I love to look at him. To me he's the most handsome man in the world—rugged yet refined features, warm, sensitive eyes, which make me melt, and soft, curly hair, which I'll remember when he goes completely bald. I knew when I met him I'd never tire of looking at him.

A second compelling attraction was his intellect. His awareness of the world around him, his broad knowledge of things political, cultural, and artistic, and his continuous love for reading and current events told me we'd never be at a loss for words. Even now, after twenty-five years together, we always have things to talk about. And I respect his intelligence, as do others around him.

Of course, your dad's wit and wacky sense of humor also exerted a strong magnetic pull. He's always made me laugh. And he's learned to temper the cynical and sarcastic parts of his humor so he's no longer hurtful.

The physical attraction that some people call chemistry has always been there with Dad, but not always to the same extent. Life's conditions exert an influence on chemistry. It's hard to find him sexy when I'm angry. It's hard to feel sexually appealing when I'm not feeling good about myself. But I believe this ebb and flow in the physical relationship between two people is natural. It's not possible to maintain the same level of intensity in an intimate relationship that is embedded in day-to-day living.

From the beginning, and reinforced over time, I've know Dad to be a good man, sensitive, loving, full of integrity, practical, and loyal. I know you'll agree he's been a great father, something difficult for him given his own family history. These are attributes I value and some of the reasons we've stayed together for twenty-five years.

Life with your dad hasn't always been easy, but it's been fun, and full, and most wonderful because of the joy you bring us. But it wasn't fate that brought us together. I chose him and he chose me. And we chose each other again, after some tough times. We choose each other every day in small ways, like when he calls me in the middle of the day to tell me about a nice phone call he got from a client or when he helps me with some jam I've gotten myself into. I choose him when I remember to check before making a social engagement or make a conscious effort not to suggest eating out when he's worried about money.

In the past we chose with our hearts and with our heads. Living together day to day means choosing with our actions.

I wish you good fortune, strength, courage, and the ability to take risks, so you too may choose with your heart and your head. Once you make a choice, I know your actions will make it true and make it work.

Mom

The secret of a
happy marriage
remains a secret.

HENNY YOUNGMAN

I will tell you the real secret of how to stay married. Keep the cave clean. They want the cave clean and spotless. Air-conditioned, if possible. Sharpen his spear, and stick it in his hand when he goes out in the morning to spear that bear; and when the bear chases him, console him when he comes home at night, and tell him what a big man he is, and then hide the spear so he doesn't fall over it and stab himself...

JEROME CHODOROV AND JOSEPH FIELDS

Your love is a great mystery.
It is like an eternal lake
whose waters are always still and clear like glass.
Looking into it you can see
the truth about your life.

It is like a deep well
whose waters are cool and pure.
Drinking from it you can be reborn.

You do not have to stir the waters
or dig the well.
Merely see yourself clearly
And drink deeply.

THE COUPLE'S TAO TE CHING: "SEE CLEARLY"
Lao Tzu

ADVICE: *A Matter of Luck*

Dear Daughter,

If you conclude that I believe marriage is largely a matter of luck, you are right. No matter what advice is provided, no matter what admonitions offered, once passion shapes your decision, it is hard to turn back. But passion does not last. Like a shooting star, passion will burn out, hopefully later rather than sooner.

Before the fire diminishes, love must flower and companionship be cultivated if a marriage is to have any chance of success. By love I mean the unrestrained desire to share, and by companionship I refer to an ease of being together. If you share what you now covet for yourself, you enhance the possibility of success. You must be willing to surrender part of yourself and become open, so emotionally transparent that your mate can read your inner thoughts. I can express these words glibly, but the conditions are difficult to achieve. The commitment in marriage is of a high order.

You are existentially selfish. I do not say this in a deprecating way. You were raised to be special, and you are. Yet I now suggest that you relinquish part of your

individuality, part of what makes you special, for your anticipated marriage. This would be an extraordinary act of generosity and the single most important display of your love.

This does not mean you must always sacrifice for your mate. In fact, slavishness undermines a relationship. But you must be prepared to sacrifice, and occasionally do so.

On life's many highways you may take a route not in total harmony with the wishes of your spouse. Without sacrificing your martial vows, you will have to find a way to retain your individual goals. This will be difficult, but weigh your sense of personal fulfillment against the pleasures of marriage, and approach your spouse willing to give. By the way, demand nothing less from him....

Remember that passion is not love, love is a necessary but insufficient condition for successful marriage, and successful marriage is most of all a function of sharing, generosity, and moderating selfish impulses. Surely you will do well. Yet if all else fails, pray. It may not guarantee success, but it will not hurt. I love you.

Dad

—FROM *FROM THE HEART*

WUTHERING HEIGHTS

By Emily Brontë

In this excerpt from Emily Brontë's classic novel, Catherine explains the depth of her love for Heathcliff, the man she truly loves but did not marry.

…HE'S MORE MYSELF THAN I AM. Whatever our souls are made of, his and mine are the same.…If all else perished and *he* remained, and he were annihilated, the universe would turn to a might stranger.…He's always, always in my mind; not as a pleasure to myself, but as my own being.

If ever two were one, then surely we.
If ever man were loved by wife, then thee;
If ever wife was happy in a man,
Compare with me ye women if you can.
I prize thy love more than whole mines of gold,
Or all the riches that the East doth hold.
My love is such that rivers cannot quench,
Nor ought but love from thee, give recompence.
Thy love is such I can no way repay,
The heavens reward thee manifold I pray.
Then while we live, in love lets so persevere,
That when we live no more, we may live ever.

TO MY DEAR AND LOVING HUSBAND
Anne Bradstreet

For ages people who've hardly known each other, let alone come to love each other, have united through the divine wisdom of match-makers and fortune-tellers. Such bonds cement families, strengthen clans, and in the case of royal marriages, seal political contracts. If a good match can be foretold in the stars, all the better.

A match made in heaven

ACCORDING TO CHINESE LORE, the gods unite each couple at birth with an invisible red cord. In time, the cord grows shorter, drawing the pair together. The pivotal role of the matchmaker is to help these predestined people find each other, according to the 3,000-year-old practice of astrology. The matchmaker evaluates a possible union on the principals of the Eight Characters or Four Pillars. She writes down characters identifying the birth hour, day, month, and year of the prospective bride and groom on rice paper. According to some practices, if the characters are lucky and if nothing bad happens in three days, the marriage can be considered a good match.

When the time comes, the matchmaker hosts a betrothal tea for the groom and his parents. The prospective bride serves the tea. If the groom wishes to pursue marriage, he will place an embroidered red satchel on his saucer. The bride may accept his offer by taking the bag. If she is not interested, she will have politely left the room before the groom has an opportunity to show his interest.

Best Matches

According to Chinese astrology, each year is represented by one of twelve animals: rat, ox, tiger, rabbit, dragon, snake, horse, goat, monkey, rooster, dog, or pig. Persons born under a certain sign are believed to take on characteristics of that animal. To figure out which animals you and your fiancé are, consult this simple chart:

RAT: 1900, 1912, 1924, 1936, 1948, 1960, 1972, 1984, 1996, 2008

OX: 1901, 1913, 1925, 1937, 1949, 1961, 1973, 1985, 1997, 2009

TIGER: 1902, 1914, 1926, 1938, 1950, 1962, 1974, 1986, 1998, 2010

HARE: 1903, 1915, 1927, 1939, 1951, 1963, 1975, 1987, 1999, 2011

DRAGON: 1904, 1916, 1928, 1940, 1952, 1964, 1976, 1988, 2000

SNAKE: 1905, 1917, 1929, 1941, 1953, 1965, 1977, 1989, 2001

HORSE: 1906, 1918, 1930, 1942, 1954, 1966, 1978, 1990, 2002

SHEEP: 1907, 1919, 1931, 1943, 1955, 1967, 1979, 1991, 2003

MONKEY: 1908, 1920, 1932, 1944, 1956, 1980, 1992, 2004

ROOSTER: 1909, 1921, 1933, 1945, 1957, 1969, 1981, 1993, 2005

DOG: 1910, 1922, 1934, 1946, 1958, 1970, 1982, 1994, 2006

PIG: 1911, 1923, 1935, 1947, 1959, 1971, 1983, 1995, 2007

Now that you know your animals, you can find out if you and your fiancé are an ideal match. Chinese matchmakers take many variables into consideration, but these pairs are sure bets for everlasting love:

 Rat & Monkey   Horse & Dog

 Ox & Rooster   Sheep & Sheep

Tiger & Horse   Monkey & Dragon

Rabbit & Sheep   Rooster & Dragon

Dragon & Rat   Dog & Tiger

Snake & Rooster   Pig & Rabbit

The spider; dropping down from twig,

Unwinds a thread of her devising:

A thin, premeditated rig

To use in rising.

And all the journey down through space,

In cool descent, and loyal-hearted,

She builds a ladder to the place

From which she started.

Thus I, gone forth, as spiders do,

In spider's web a truth discerning,

Attach one silken strand to you

For my returning.

NATURAL HISTORY
E. B. White

Chains do not hold
a marriage together.
It is threads, hundreds
of tiny threads which
sew people together
through the years.
That is what makes
a marriage last.

SIMONE SIGNORET

I had just completed the full cycle of initiation at the age of sixteen when I was called into the circle of the elders, and I was quite surprised. One can never guess why the elders call one into their circle, but one thing is sure: their cooking pot always has something boiling in it.

At any rate, when I got there, they said, "Well, we have this son who lives in the West, and we need somebody who can keep him company." My answer was "What does that have to do with me?" And their response was "You see, you are the kind of person who can get along with him. We would like you to marry him." I said, "Well, isn't there anybody else in the village who can get along with him?"

INITIATION

BY SOBONFU SOMÉ

My ambivalence about leaving the village led me to a state of confusion, which in turn confused the elders, who did not know what to tell me. The only thing they said was "Your life purpose, Sobonfu, is on the same road as his. We're not trying to force you to marry somebody, because we know that being far away from home is very difficult. If he lived somewhere around here, we wouldn't have even called you here. We wouldn't have had this meeting and given you a choice. You would have simply been notified."

So I said, "How am I going to live far away and be able to survive without my family and without everybody else?" And they said, "You are going to be taken care of. You just need to give us your yes, and then everything will be fine." And I said, "Well, I can't give you my answer right now because I don't know what I'm dealing with." So they said, "Well, you have some time. Go think about it, and come back and tell us what you think."

I thought about it for three months. First I went to my parents and said, "What do you think I should do?" They said, "No. You can't ask us. We are too attached to this issue to give you good advice." My grandmother had just passed away, and she had been my main counselor. After a month I went to my other grandmothers, and they said that they, too, were too attached to give me any kind of advice.

And so I spent some time around my grandmother's grave. One night, as I was sitting on her grave, these words came to me: "Don't worry. Just say yes, and you'll see that everything will be fine." And so the next day I woke up, and I went to the elders and said yes.

They were quite relieved, and they said, "We'll start everything, and the wedding will be on its way." I didn't know Malidoma, my future husband, but I knew his family. He was the only person in his family that I didn't know. So the wedding came when I was twenty, and since, in the village, you do not need to be at your wedding, Malidoma wasn't there. He was notified by mail afterward.

Malidoma had been sent to the West by the elders to teach their wisdom and to become, as his name describes, "a friend of the stranger." He had studied first at the University of Ouagadougou in Burkina Faso and then at the Sorbonne in France, after which he ended up in America. At the time of our wedding he was in America, at Brandeis University in Massachusetts.

Malidoma saved enough money to buy himself a ticket, and a year later he came home and we met. We were introduced as a couple. We didn't know each other, and we wondered how in the world we were going to make anything happen. Now, one of the things that I had learned from the elders in initiation was how to create a sacred space, and how to build an intimate relationship in that space. As Malidoma and I spent time together, we started to work on that issue.

In the village, women and men do not sleep together. Though they share the same compound, women sleep in their quarters, and men sleep in their quarters, and that is because, in order to bring their strength to society, they need to empower one another; they need to bring one another's best out so that whenever a woman goes out to meet with the man, there isn't an imbalance created.

The first thing that people want to know when they hear of this sleeping arrangement is how a couple manages to get together. I tell them that as long as they keep their creativity and imagination alive, they will figure it out.

Malidoma came home, and at the time I was sleeping with his mother. His mother and I used to share the same bed. You can understand how frustrating the idea of being married to a woman who sleeps with your mother can be to the Western mind. For me what was harder was being in a sacred place with Malidoma, someone I did not know. There was something strange about it. So I surrendered to spirits, letting them figure it out. All I needed to do when I felt frustrated was to create a sacred space.

The way we created sacred space in the village was just by using ash to make a circle. You bring an earthen pot full of water, and you put it in the middle of the circle. Whoever starts the ritual will sit and wait for the other person to come. When the other person gets there, then you do an invocation, and as you invoke the spirit, something inside automatically unlocks itself.

Malidoma and I were strangers to each other, but each time we met in that space, it was as if we had known each other forever.

Let there be spaces in your togetherness.

KAHLIL GIBRAN

Though you know it anyhow
Listen to me, darling, now,

Proving what I need not prove
How I know I love you, love.

Near and far, near and far,
I am happy where you are;

Likewise I have never learnt
How to be it where you aren't.

Far and wide, far and wide,
I can walk with you beside;

Furthermore, I tell you what,
I sit and sulk where you are not.

Visitors remark my frown
When you're upstairs and I am down,

Yes, and I'm afraid I pout
When I'm indoors and you are out;

But how contentedly I view
Any room containing you.

In fact I care not where you be,
Just as long as it's with me.

In all your absences I glimpse
Fire and flood and trolls and imps.

Is your train a minute slothful?
I goad the stationmaster wrothful.

When with friends to bridge you drive
I never know if you're alive,

And when you linger late in shops
I long to telephone the cops.

Yet how worth the waiting for,
To see you coming through the door.

Somehow, I can be complacent
Never but with you adjacent.

Near and far, near and far,
I am happy where you are;

Likewise, I have never learnt
How to be it where you aren't.

Then grudge me not my fond endeavor,
To hold you in my sight forever;

Let none, not even you, disparage
Such valid reason for a marriage.

THE WEDDING WHISTLE
Ogden Nash

A family starts with a young man falling in love with a girl. No superior alternative has been found.

WINSTON CHURCHILL

THE RAINBOW

BY D.H. LAWRENCE

Set on the Derbyshire-Nottinghamshire border, D. H. Lawrence's The Rainbow *chronicles the lives of three generations of the Brangwen family. The story opens with Tom Brangwen, who, after many long February nights, is ready to seek the hand of the vicar's housekeeper, a Polish widow named Lydia Lensky.*

"I CAME UP," HE SAID, speaking curiously matter-of-fact and level, "to ask if you'd marry me. You are free, aren't you?"

There was a long silence, whilst his blue eyes, strangely impersonal, looked into her eyes to seek an answer to the truth. He was looking for the truth out of her. And she, as if hypnotized, must answer at length.

"Yes, I am free to marry."

The expression of his eyes changed, became less impersonal, as if he were looking almost at her, for the truth of her. Steady and intent and eternal they were, as if they would never change. They seemed to fix and to resolve her. She quivered, feeling herself created, will-less, lapsing into him, into a common will with him.

"You want me?" she said.

A pallor came over his face.

"Yes," he said.

Still there was suspense and silence.

"No," she said, not of herself. "No, I don't know."

He felt the tension breaking up in him, his fists slackened, he was unable to move. He stood looking at her, helpless in his vague collapse. For the moment she had become unreal to him. Then he saw her come to him, curiously direct and as if without movement, in a sudden flow. She put her hand to his coat.

"Yes, I want to," she said impersonally, looking at him with wide, candid, newly-opened eyes, opened now with supreme truth. He went very white as he stood, and did not move, only his eyes were held by hers, and he suffered. She seemed to see him with her newly-opened, wide eyes, almost of a child, and with a strange movement, that was agony to him, she reached slowly forward her dark face and her breast to him, with a slow insinuation of a kiss that made something break in his brain, and it was darkness over him for a few moments.

He had her in his arms, and, obliterated, was kissing her. And it was sheer, blenched agony to him, to break away from himself. She was there so small and light and accepting in his arms, like a child, and yet with such an insinuation of embrace, of infinite embrace, that he could not bear it, he could not stand.

He turned and looked for a chair, and keeping her still in his arms, sat down with her close to him, to his breast. Then, for a few seconds, he went utterly to sleep, asleep and sealed in the darkest sleep, utter, extreme oblivion.

The best way to hold
a man is in your arms.

MAE WEST

Say you'll be mine

A candlelight dinner for two; a walk in the park hand in hand; a delivery of long-stemmed red roses. Ah, sweet romance! Dating customs of love-smitten men have ranged from the boisterous to the sublime— and have been, in some cases, less than virtuous! While your wedding may signify the end of courtship, it certainly does not mean the death of romance. Find inspiration in the following wooing traditions and keep your marriage full of passion.

THE ART OF SHOWERING one's true love with poems and serenades did not fade with Romeo and Juliet. Affection-seeking gentlemen in Spain, Brazil, and the Philippines still take this tradition very seriously. They hope to win the hearts of their beloved with verses they've composed themselves. Often they'll invite a group of friends to accompany them with musical instruments while they sing and dance until the wee hours of the morning.

IN MID-TWENTIETH-CENTURY AMERICA, the custom of dating involved time spent together on the porch swing or going to a drive-in movie. But during colonial times, couples courted between the sheets! English and Dutch emigrants from rural communities introduced this custom, called bundling, which was touted as a way to save on heating costs. Families permitted wooing couples to get to know each other—fully or partially dressed—in bed. A "bundling board" placed in the bed was supposed to separate the lovebirds and keep them chaste. Preventive measures weren't always failsafe, however, resulting in more than one pregnant bride at the altar....

How does a woman show that her heart belongs to someone? By spooning with her sweetheart, of course. What has come to be known as necking or snuggling got its start from an old Welsh custom. A man would woo his beloved with an elaborately carved wooden spoon. If she accepted his affections, she would attach it to a ribbon and wear it around her neck as a sign of betrothal.

In rural Poland, a man might show his feelings for a woman by visiting her and inquiring about purchasing a horse. If, during their conversation, he reveals a bottle of vodka wrapped in red ribbons and flowers, she'll know the visit has nothing to do with her horse. Instead of asking for her hand in marriage, he'll simply ask for a glass. If she is ready to be his bride, she'll return with glasses and her family to celebrate their betrothal.

IN MANY AFRICAN VILLAGES, courtship is not between two people, but between two families. If a prospective suitor wishes to inquire about a certain unwed female, he might send his mother, aunt, or other married female relative to knock on her family's door. She asks to arrange a meeting of family members and village elders. The prospective suitor will bring gifts of money, grain, produce, and livestock to show his ability to provide for his new bride and future family.

War of the Posies

In England, suitors were mad about flowers, especially during Victorian times, when virtually everything that bloomed carried a special symbolism. When a young man wished to gain the affection of a certain young woman, he would send her posies that held secret messages. She would reply in kind with specific flowers that would either welcome or shun his attentions. Here's a sampling of petal lore:

Ambrosia— "Love returned"

Burdock— "Touch me not"

Camellia— "You are perfected loveliness"

Currant— "Thy frown will kill me"

Daffodil— "Unrequited love"

Narcissus— "Uncertainty"

Pansies— "Think of me"

Peach blossoms— "Am I your captive?"

Pink rose— "Our love is perfect happiness"

Ranunculus— "You are radiant with charm"

Red columbine— "Anxious and trembling"

Wild daisy— "I will think of it"

The following article was originally published in People Magazine, *January 26, 1998.*

Skywriting? Been done. Engagement ring on the lobster claw? Boring. What Bill Gottlieb was searching for was the *perfect* way to propose to his sweetheart, Emily Mindel. And that's when Gottlieb got a clue. "Emily does the puzzle every day," said the twenty-seven-year-old New York City corporate lawyer, referring to the venerable *New York Times* crossword. "I thought that would be a romantic way to propose." So last October, Gottlieb called *Times* puzzle editor Will Shortz and asked him to play Cupid. "My reaction was, 'Wow, what a great idea!'" says Shortz, who agreed to weave a wedding proposal into the puzzle as "a onetime thing."

LOVE AND LETTERS

ALEX TRESNIOWSKI AND HELENE STAPINSKI

The puzzle ran on January 7. Gottlieb invited Mindel, a Brooklyn Law School student, to brunch. "I just said, 'Let's grab the paper,'" he recalls. "Very casual. But I was so nervous." Gottlieb feigned interest in the rest of the paper while Mindel, twenty-four and a crossword whiz, penciled in answers: 38 Across asked for a Gary Lewis and the Playboys hit ("This Diamond Ring"); 56 Across was a Paula Abdul song ("Will You Marry Me"). Other answers included "Emily," "BillG," and "Yes" (the hoped-for response to 56 Across). "I had the feeling the puzzle was saying something," says Mindel, no dummy. "My heart was racing, and I got all hot and flushed."

With only four squares undone, Mindel faced her beau and stammered, "This puzzle…" over and over.

"Her voice was all shaky," he says. "I smiled and asked, "Will you marry me?" Mindel's reply: an eight-letter phrase for *absolutely* ("Of course!"). Now the couple, fixed up by their families in 1995, are shopping for a ring and planning an intimate wedding (Shortz is on the guest list). When's the big day? Umm, they haven't a clue.

ANNA KARENINA

By Leo Tolstoy

Anna Karenina, set in mid–nineteenth–century Russia, is an emotional tale filled with love, longing, and heartbreak. A love triangle unfolds as Kitty is courted by two men, Levin and Vronsky. After choosing Vronsky, he betrays her by falling in love with another woman. Distraught and alone, Kitty falls ill and Levin retires to his country estate. But when Kitty and Levin are finally reunited, love blossoms.

SHE SAW HIM THE INSTANT HE ENTERED THE ROOM. She had been waiting for him. She was filled with joy, and so confused at her own joy, that there was a moment—the moment when he went up to his hostess and glanced again at her—when she, and he, and Dolly, who saw it all, thought she would break down and burst into tears. Blushing and going pale by turns, she sat rigid, waiting with quivering lips for his approach. He went up to her, bowed, and silently held out his hand. Except for the slight quiver of her lips and the moist film that came over her eyes, making them appear brighter, her smile was almost calm as she said:

"What a long time it is since we met!" and with desperate resolve her cold hand pressed his.

They resumed the conversation started at dinner-the emancipation and occupations of women. Levin agreed with Dolly that a girl who did not marry could always find some feminine occupation in the family. He supported this view by saying that no family can get along without women to help them, that every family, poor or rich, had to have nurses, either paid or belonging to the family.

"No," said Kitty, blushing, but looking at him all the more boldly with her truthful eyes, "a girl may be so placed that it is humiliating for her to live in the family, while she herself…"

He understood her allusion.

"Oh yes," he said. "Yes, yes, yes—you're right; you're right!"

And he saw all that Pestsov had been driving at at dinner about the freedom of women, simply because he got a glimpse of the terror in Kitty's heart of the humiliation of remaining an old maid; and, loving her, he felt that terror and humiliation, and at once gave up his contention.

A silence followed. She continued scribbling on the table with the chalk. Her eyes shone with a soft light. Surrendering to her mood he felt a continually growing tension of happiness throughout his whole being.

"Oh, I've scribbled all over the table!" she exclaimed, and, putting down the chalk, made a movement to get up.

"What! Shall I be left alone—without her?" he thought, with terror, and took the piece of chalk. "Don't go," he said, sitting down at the table. "I've wanted to ask you a question for a long time." He looked straight into her caressing, though frightened eyes.

"What is it?"

"Here," he said, and wrote down the initial letters, w, y, t, m, *i, c, n, b*—d, t, m, n, o, t? These letters stood for, "When you told me *it could not be*—did that mean never, or then?" There seemed no likelihood that she would be able to decipher this complicated sequence; but he looked at her as though his life depended on her understanding the words.

She gazed up at him seriously, then leaned her puckered forehead on her hand and began to read. Once or twice she stole a look at him, as though asking, "Is it what I think?"

"I know what it is," she said flushing a little.

"What is this word?" he asked, pointing to the *n* which stood for *never*.

"That means *never*," she said, "but it's not true!"

He quickly rubbed out what he had written, handed her the chalk, and stood up. She wrote: *T, I, c, n, a, d.*

Dolly felt consoled for the grief caused by her conversation with Karenin when she caught sight of the two together: Kitty with the chalk in her hand, gazing up at Levin with a shy, happy smile, and his fine figure bending over the table, his radiant eyes directed now on the table, now on her. He was suddenly radiant: he had understood. The letters meant: "Then I could not answer differently."

He glanced at her questioningly, timidly.

"Only then?"

"Yes," her smile answered.

"And n...—and now?" he asked.

"Well, read this. I'll tell you what I should like, what I should like so much!" She wrote the initial letters: *i, y, c, f, a, f, w, h,* meaning, "If you could forget and forgive what happened."

He seized the chalk, breaking it with his nervous, trembling fingers, and wrote the first letters of the following sentence: "I have nothing to forget and forgive; I have never ceased to love you."

She looked at him with a smile that did not waver.

"I understand," she said in a whisper.

He sat down and wrote a long sentence. She understood it all and, without asking if she was right, took the chalk and at once wrote the answer.

For a long time he could not make out what it was, and kept looking up into her eyes. He was dazed with happiness. He could not fill in the words she meant at all; but in her lovely eyes, suffused with happiness, he saw all he needed to know. And he wrote down three letters. But before he had finished writing she read them over his arm, and herself finished and wrote the answer, "Yes."

I go about murmuring, 'I have made that dignified girl commit herself, I have, I have,' and then I vault over the sofa with exultation.

WALTER BAGEHOT
(MARRIED HIS LOVE ELIZABETH WILSON IN 1858)

My Dear Miss,

I now take up my pen to write to you hoping these few lines will find you well as it leaves me at present Thank God for it. You will perhaps be surprised that I should make so bold as to write to you who is such a lady and I hope you will not be vex at me for it. I hardly dare say what I want, I am so timid about ladies, and my heart trimmels like a hespin. But I once seed in a book that faint heart never won fair lady, so here goes.

HOPEFUL PROPOSAL TO A YOUNG LADY OF THE VILLAGE

A REAL PROPOSAL LETTER
BY SIMON FALLOWFIELD

I am a farmer in a small way and my age is rather more than forty years and my mother lives with me and keeps my house, and she has been very poorly lately and cannot stir about much and I think I should be more comfortabler with a wife.

I have had my eye on you a long time and I think you are a very nice young woman and one that would make me happy if only you think so. We keep a servant girl to milk three kye and do the work in the house, and she goes on a bit in the summer to gadder wickens and she snags a few of turnips in the back kend. I do a piece of work on the farm myself and attends Pately Market, and I sometimes show a few sheep and I feeds between 3 & 4 pigs agen Christmas, and the same is very useful in the house to make pies and cakes and so forth, and I sells the hams to help pay for the barley meal.

I have about 73 pund in Naisbro Bank and we have a nice little parlour downstairs with a blue carpet, and an oven on the side of the fireplace and the old woman on the other side smoking. The Golden Rules claimed up on the walls above the long settle, and you could sit all day in the easy chair and knit and mend my kytles and leggums, and you could make the tea ready agin I come in, and you could make butter for Pately Market, and I would drive you to church every Sunday in the spring cart, and I would do all that bees in my power to make you happy. So I hope to hear from you. I am in desprit and Yurnest, and will marry you at May Day, or if my mother dies afore I shall want you afore. If only you will accept of me, my dear, we could be very happy together.

I hope you will let me know your mind by return of post, and if you are favourable I will come up to scratch. So no more at present from your well-wisher and true love—

Simon Fallowfield

P.S. I hope you will say nothing about this. If you will not accept of me I have another very nice woman in my eye, and I think I shall marry her if you do not accept of me, but I thought you would suit me mother better, she being very crusty at times. So I tell you now before you come, she will be Maister.

THIS PROPOSAL WAS REFUSED BY MARY FOSTER, THE LOCAL BEAUTY OF MIDDLEMOOR, PATELY BRIDGE, IN YORKSHIRE.

My most brilliant achievement was my ability to be able to persuade my wife to marry me.

WINSTON CHURCHILL

Do you  all for me, and my Love is as soft as an For you Hair and of my eye, so if we anyhow, for I know we w

for my heart  for you

as a but as strong

are a with your

nose. You are the

then marry,

uld make a happy

Come live with me and be my love,
And we will all the pleasures prove
That hills and valleys, dales and fields
And all the craggy mountains yields.

There we will sit upon the rocks
And see the shepherds feed their flocks,
By shallow rivers to whose falls
Melodious birds sing madrigals.

And I will make thee beds of roses
With a thousand fragrant posies,
A cap of flowers and a kirtle
Embroidered all with leaves of myrtle.

A gown made of the finest wool
Which from our pretty lambs we pull;
Fair lined slippers for the cold,
With buckles of the purest gold;

A belt of straw and ivy buds,
With coral clasps and amber studs:
And if these pleasures may thee move,
Come live with me and be my love.

The shepherds' swains shall dance
   and sing
For thy delight each May morning:
If these delights thy mind may move,
Then live with me and be my love.

THE PASSIONATE SHEPHERD
TO HIS LOVE
Christopher Marlowe

*Y*ou're engaged! It's unmistakable: Friends and strangers alike know it's official when they see an engagement ring on your finger. But how did the ring become a symbol of marital unity?

This ring is round and hath no end

IN ANCIENT ROME, husbands promised commitment to their wives with rings made of iron. Those too poor to afford a ring would seal their engagement with the loop of a door key to the new marital home. Some of the earliest rings were not metal at all, but made of woven grasses or leather. Others were carved out of ivory or bone. In A.D. 860, Pope Nicholas I decreed a new mandate for the Catholic world to ensure that engagements would be binding: From then on, the ring was not only a requirement for nuptial intent but should be made of a valuable metal, preferably gold.

ANCIENT EGYPTIANS BELIEVED the ring, a perfect circle, represented a supernatural link to eternal love shared by two people. This is just one of the many shades of cultural meaning that rings have had throughout the history of marriage.

So is my love unto my friend

THROUGHOUT MEDIEVAL TIMES, the betrothal ring was also used as a wedding ring. It is not until the fifteenth century that both a betrothal and wedding ring were given. Historically, men have chosen not to wear wedding rings; it was not until the popularity of the gimmal ring in the sixteenth century that they began to embrace the idea. Double-ring ceremonies became fashionable in the United States during World War II, as the ring became a tangible link to home for young husbands posted overseas. The custom has endured to the present.

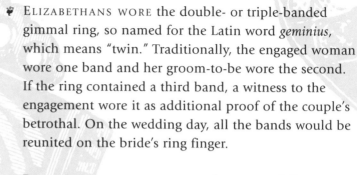

❧ ELIZABETHANS WORE the double- or triple-banded gimmal ring, so named for the Latin word *geminius*, which means "twin." Traditionally, the engaged woman wore one band and her groom-to-be wore the second. If the ring contained a third band, a witness to the engagement wore it as additional proof of the couple's betrothal. On the wedding day, all the bands would be reunited on the bride's ring finger.

❧ RENOWNED FOR THEIR LOVE of poetry and flowers, the Elizabethans exchanged poesy rings with mottoes or poetic love couplets known as poesies engraved on the inside or outside of the band.

❧ USUALLY HANDED DOWN from mother to daughter in Ireland, the Claddagh ring features two hands holding a crowned heart. The crown is worn so that it points toward the wrist on betrothal; upon marriage, the wearer turns the ring around so that the crown faces outward.

❧ THE CELTIC LOVE-KNOT RING, a symbol of eternity, unity, and fidelity, is made of intertwined, unending lines.

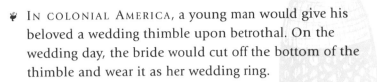

♥ IN COLONIAL AMERICA, a young man would give his beloved a wedding thimble upon betrothal. On the wedding day, the bride would cut off the bottom of the thimble and wear it as her wedding ring.

♥ IN FRANCE, it is customary to engrave the bride's name and half of the wedding date on one wedding band and the groom's name and the other half of the date on the other ring. The names and wedding date then come together as the rings are slipped onto the finger during the ceremony.

♥ IN THE 1870s, Tiffany & Co. designed the first ring with the tone set above the band. This famous Tiffany setting has come to epitomize the modern engagement ring.

♥ AN OLD IRISH TRADITION had the man presenting his intended with a woven bracelet of human hair as a symbol of his unending love.

♥ VICTORIANS LOVED to spell messages with gemstones in their rings. For example, Ruby, Emerald, Garnet, Amethyst, Ruby, Diamond says "regard," while Lapis lazuli, Opal, Verde antique, Emerald spells "love."

Which Finger?

To know if a woman is married, simply look for a ring at the third finger on her left hand, right? Ancient Egyptians did so, but that was not necessarily the norm for everyone. In Ancient Rome, women commonly wore rings on their thumbs. Medieval Gauls and Britons wore rings on their little fingers. And in sixteenth-century England, women wore rings on their right hands. Some Jewish wedding rings are so ornate they're too bulky to wear at all. These rings symbolize the holy temple and serve as ceremonial pieces only, such as a holder for the bride's bouquet.

Perhaps one reason why the third finger of the left hand remains the finger of choice has to do with an old but mistaken belief about anatomy. According to lore, a vein from that finger, aptly named vena amoris, leads directly to the heart. Putting a ring on that finger would keep love from escaping the body.

There's also the medieval Trinitarian formula: During Christian wedding ceremonies, the ring would be placed on the thumb, "in the name of the Father;" on the index finger, "in the name of the Son;" on the middle finger, "in the name of the Holy Spirit;" and, last, on the third finger, "Amen."

On a more practical note, a ring worn on the third finger of the left hand is less likely to get damaged—if you're right-handed.

For years my wedding ring
has done its job. It has led me
not into temptation. It has
reminded my husband
numerous times at parties
that it's time to go home.
It has been a source of relief
to a dinner companion.
It has been a status symbol in
the maternity ward.

ERMA BOMBECK

A PROPOSALE

BY DAISY ASHFORD

Written by Daisy Ashford when she was just a little girl, and published years later, in 1919, with the original spelling and punctuation intact.

NEXT MORNING while imbibing his morning tea beneath his pink silken quilt Bernard decided he must marry Ethel with no more delay. I love the girl he said to himself and she must be mine but I somehow feel I can not propose in London it would not be seemly in the city of London. We must go for a day in the country and when surrounded by the gay twittering of the birds and the smell of the cows I will lay my suit at her feet and he waved his arm wildly at the gay thought. Then he sprang from bed and gave a rat tat at Ethel's door.

Are you up my dear he called.

Well not quite said Ethel hastilly jumping from her downy nest.

Be quick cried Bernard I have a plan to spend a day near Windsor Castle and we will take our lunch and spend a happy day.

Oh Hurrah shouted Ethel I shall soon be ready as I had my bath last night so wont wash very much now.

No dont said Bernard and added in a rarther fervent tone through the chink of the door you are fresher than the rose my dear no soap could make you fairer.

Then he dashed off very embarrased to dress. Ethel blushed and felt a bit excited as she heard the words and she put on a new white muslin dress in a fit of high spirits. She looked very beautifull with some red roses in her hat and the dainty red ruge in her cheeks looked quite the thing. Bernard heaved a sigh and his eyes flashed as he beheld her and Ethel thorght to herself what a fine type of manhood he reprisented with his nice thin legs in pale broun trousers and well fitting spats and a red rose in his button hole and rarther a sporting cap which gave him a great air with its quaint check and little flaps to pull down if necessary. Off they started the envy of all the waiters.

They arrived at Windsor very hot from the jorney and Bernard at once hired a boat to row his beloved up the river. Ethel could not row but she much enjoyed seeing the tough sunburnt arms of Bernard tugging at the oars as she lay among the rich cushons of the dainty boat. She had a rarther lazy nature but Bernard did not know of this. However he soon got dog tired and sugested lunch by the mossy bank.

Oh yes said Ethel quickly opening the sparkling champaigne.

Dont spill any cried Bernard as he carved some chicken.

They eat and drank deeply of the charming viands ending up with merangs and choclates.

Let us now bask under the spreading trees said Bernard in a passiunate tone.

Oh yes lets said Ethel and she opened her dainty parasole and sank down upon the long green grass. She closed her eyes but she was far from asleep. Bernard sat beside her in profound silence gazing at her pink face and long wavy eye lashes. He puffed at his pipe for some moments while the larks gaily caroled in the blue sky. Then he edged a trifle closer to Ethels form.

Ethel he murmured in a trembly voice.

Oh what is it said Ethel hastily sitting up.

Words fail me ejaculated Bernard horsly my passion for you is intense he added fervently. It has grown day and night since I first beheld you.

Oh said Ethel in susprise I am not prepared for this and she lent back against the trunk of the tree.

Bernard placed one arm tightly round her. When will you marry me Ethel he uttered you must be my wife it has come to that I love you so intensly that if you say no I shall perforce dash my body to the brink of yon muddy river he panted wildly.

Oh dont do that implored Ethel breathing rarther hard.

Then say you love me he cried.

Oh Bernard she sighed fervently I certinly love you madly you are to me like a Heathen god she cried looking at his manly form and handsome flashing face I will indeed marry you.

How soon gasped Bernard gazing at her intensly.

As soon as possible said Ethel gently closing her eyes.

My Darling whispered Bernard and he seiezed her in his arms we will be marrid next week.

Oh Bernard muttered Ethel this is so sudden.

No no cried Bernard and taking the bull by both horns he kissed her violently on her dainty face. My bride to be he murmered several times.

Ethel trembled with joy as she heard the mistick words.

Oh Bernard she said little did I ever dream of such as this and she suddenly fainted into his out stretched arms.

Oh I say gasped Bernard and laying the dainty burden on the grass he dashed to the waters edge and got a cup full of the fragrant river to pour on his true loves pallid brow.

She soon came to and looked up with a sickly smile Take me back to the Gaierty hotel she whispered faintly.

With plesure my darling said Bernard I will just pack up our viands ere I unloose the boat.

Ethel felt better after a few drops of champagne and began to tidy her hair while Bernard packed the remains of the food. Then arm in arm they tottered to the boat.

I trust you have not got an illness my darling murmered Bernard as he helped her in.

Oh no I am very strong said Ethel I fainted from joy she added to explain matters.

Oh I see said Bernard handing her a cushon well some people do he added kindly and so saying they rowed down the dark stream now flowing silently beneath a golden moon. All was silent as the lovers glided home with joy in their hearts and radiance on their faces only the sound of the mystearious water lapping against the frail vessel broke the monotony of the night.

Julia, I bring
To thee this ring,
  Made for thy finger fit;
To show by this
That our love is
  Or should be, like to it.

Loose though it be,
The joint is free;
  So, when love's yoke is on,
It must not gall,
Nor fret at all,
  With hard oppression.

But it must play,
Still either way,
  And be, too, such a yoke
As not too wide
To overslide,
  Or be so straight to choke.

So we who bear
This beam, must rear
  Ourselves to such a height
As that the stay
Of either may
  Create the burthen light.

And as this round
Is nowhere found
  To flaw, or else to sever,
So let our love
As endless prove,
  And pure as gold forever.

TO JULIA
Robert Herrick

Diamonds are a girl's best friend

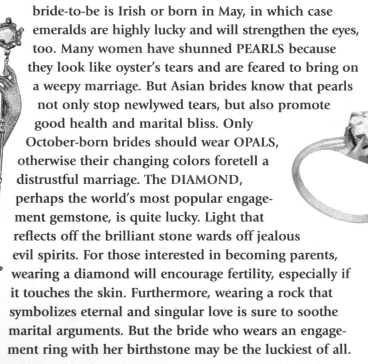

What's in a stone? Fortune or misfortune, depending on whom you ask. The "true blue" SAPPHIRE promises marital happiness. But the unlucky EMERALD spells jealousy for its wearer, unless the bride-to-be is Irish or born in May, in which case emeralds are highly lucky and will strengthen the eyes, too. Many women have shunned PEARLS because they look like oyster's tears and are feared to bring on a weepy marriage. But Asian brides know that pearls not only stop newlywed tears, but also promote good health and marital bliss. Only October-born brides should wear OPALS, otherwise their changing colors foretell a distrustful marriage. The DIAMOND, perhaps the world's most popular engagement gemstone, is quite lucky. Light that reflects off the brilliant stone wards off jealous evil spirits. For those interested in becoming parents, wearing a diamond will encourage fertility, especially if it touches the skin. Furthermore, wearing a rock that symbolizes eternal and singular love is sure to soothe marital arguments. But the bride who wears an engagement ring with her birthstone may be the luckiest of all.

MONTH	STONE	SYMBOLISM
JANUARY	GARNET	CONSTANCY, FIDELITY
FEBRUARY	AMETHYST	SINCERITY
MARCH	AQUAMARINE	COURAGE
APRIL	DIAMOND	INNOCENCE, PURITY
MAY	EMERALD	HAPPINESS, SUCCESS IN LOVE
JUNE	PEARL	BEAUTY
JULY	RUBY	LOVE, CLARITY OF HEART
AUGUST	PERIDOT	JOY
SEPTEMBER	SAPPHIRE	WISDOM, FAITHFULNESS
OCTOBER	OPAL	CONSISTENCY, FEARLESSNESS
NOVEMBER	TOPAZ	FIDELITY
DECEMBER	TURQUOISE	SUCCESS, PROSPERITY

Dear Corliss,

 It was so nice to see you again. I would have liked to have a long talk with you and would like to now. Apparently I am going to marry Charles Lindbergh. It must seem hysterically funny to you as it did to me, when

BRING ME A UNICORN:
DIARIES AND LETTERS OF
ANNE MORROW LINDBERGH 1922–1928.

I consider my opinions on marriage. "A safe marriage," "things in common," "liking the same things," "a quiet life," etc., etc.—All those things which I am apparently going against. But they seem—to have lost their meaning, or have other definitions. Isn't it funny—*why does* one marry, anyway? I didn't expect or want anything like this. I think probably that was the trouble. It must be fatal to decide on the kind of man you *don't* want to marry and the kind of life you *don't* want to lead. You determinedly turn your back on it, set out in the opposite direction—and come bang up against it, in true *Alice in the Looking Glass* fashion. And there he is—darn it all—the great Western strong-man-open-spaces type and a life of relentless action! But after all, what am I going to do about it? After all, there he is and I've got to go. I wish I could hurry up and get it over

with soon. This horrible, fantastic, absurd publicity and thousands of people telling me how lucky and happy I am.

Corliss, if you write me and wish me conventional happiness, I will *never* forgive you. Don't wish me happiness—I don't expect to be happy, but it's gotten beyond that, somehow. Wish me courage and strength and a sense of humor—I will need them all.

Funny, my writing to you this way. But I could not write you a conventional "He-is-just-fine" letter. I feel as if I knew you so well. Corliss, you will not show this or quote it to anyone, will you? It would be awful if it got into the papers—as everything seems to. I don't mind if you tell Margaret, for I trust her and like her.

I can't leave this with an utterly frivolous picture of him. He is so much more than that. But talking about a person is almost always futile. Just reserve your opinions, Corliss, until you meet him. Newspaper accounts, casual acquaintance opinions, friendly articles about him are so utterly wrong.

He has vision and a sense of humor and extraordinarily nice eyes!

And that is enough to say now.

In our life there is a single color,
as on an artist's palette, which provides
the meaning of life and art. It is the
color of love.

MARC CHAGALL

HOWARD'S END

By E. M. Forster

Set in England in the early 20th century, Howards End *is the story of two wealthy families divided by their ideals but brought together by circumstance. After the loss of his wife, the conservative Mr. Wilcox develops an unlikely fondess for the young, liberated Margaret Schlegel and dares to propose marriage.*

THEY PROCEEDED TO THE DRAWING-ROOM....One could visualize the ladies withdrawing to it, while their lords discussed life's realities below, to the accompaniment of cigars....

Just as this thought entered Margaret's brain, Mr. Wilcox did ask her to be his wife, and the knowledge that she had been right so overcame her that she nearly fainted.

But the proposal was not to rank among the world's great love scenes.

"Miss Schlegel"—his voice was firm—"I have had you up on false pretenses. I want to speak about a much more serious matter than a house."

Margaret almost answered: "I know—"

"Could you be induced to share my—is it probable—"

"Oh, Mr. Wilcox!" she interrupted, holding the piano and averting her eyes. "I see, I see. I will write to you afterwards if I may."

He began to stammer. "Miss Schlegel—Margaret—you don't understand."

"Oh, yes! Indeed, yes!" said Margaret.

"I am asking you to be my wife."

So deep already was her sympathy, that when he said, "I am asking you to be my wife," she made herself give a little start. She must show surprise if he expected it. An immense joy came over her. It was indescribable. It had nothing to do with humanity, and most resembled the all-pervading happiness of fine weather. Fine weather is due to the sun, but Margaret could think of no central radiance here. She stood in his drawing-room happy, and longing to give happiness. On leaving him she realized that the central radiance had been love.

"You aren't offended, Miss Schlegel?"

"How could I be offended?"

There was a moment's pause. He was anxious to get rid of her, and she knew it. She had too much intuition to look at him as he struggled for possessions that money cannot buy. He desired comradeship and affection, but he feared them, and she, who had taught herself only to desire, and could have clothed the struggle with beauty, held back, and hesitated with him.

"Good-bye," she continued. "You will have a letter from me—I am going back to Swanage tomorrow."

"Thank you."

"Good-bye, and it's you I thank."

"I may order the motor round, mayn't I?"

"That would be most kind."

"I wish I had written instead. Ought I to have written?"

"Not at all."

"There's just one question—"

She shook her head. He looked a little bewildered, and they parted.

They parted without shaking hands: she had kept the interview, for his sake, in tints of the quietest gray. Yet she thrilled with happiness ere she reached her own house. Others had loved her in the past, if one may apply to their brief desires so grave a word, but those others had been "ninnies"— young men who had nothing to do, old men who could find nobody better. And she had often "loved," too, but only so far as the facts of sex demanded: mere yearnings for the masculine, to be dismissed for what they were worth, with a smile. Never before had her personality been touched. She was not young or very rich, and it amazed her that a man of any standing should take her seriously. As she sat trying to do accounts in her empty house, amidst beautiful pictures and noble books, waves of emotion broke, as if a tide of passion was flowing through the night air. She shook her head, tried to concentrate her attention, and failed. In vain did she repeat: "But I've been through this sort of thing before." She had never been through it; the big machinery, as opposed to the little, had been set in motion, and the idea that Mr. Wilcox loved, obsessed her before she came to love him in return.

ENGAGEMENT COCKTAIL PARTY

Often hosted by the bride and groom or their families, a stylish and love-themed cocktail soirée is a simple yet elegant way to celebrate your engagement. Our recipes for champagne punch and delicious heart shaped hors d'oeuvres are the perfect accompaniments for a night of romance. Just add a little Sinatra in the background, tons of candles, some gorgeous flowers and enjoy the moment.

CHAMPAGNE PUNCH

½ cup sugar
1 pineapple, chopped
1 cup fresh lemon juice
1 cup fresh orange juice
2 cups light rum
⅔ cup Cointreau
⅔ cup grenadine
2 bottles champagne, chilled
2 cups ice
Mint leaves and thin orange slices for garnish

1. Combine sugar and pineapple in a large punch bowl. Set aside for 1 hour.

2. Add lemon juice, orange juice, rum, Cointreau and grenadine. Chill for 2 hours.

3. Right before serving add champagne and ice. Garnish each glass with orange slice and mint sprig.

Serves 8-10

LOVELY HORS D'OEUVRES

Delicious and delightful, these sweet heart shaped finger sandwiches are the perfect accompaniment to the Champagne punch. For the toast, we recommend using a loaf of Italian bread (Ciabatta is good) from any gourmet deli, though regular sandwich bread will work, as well. Prepare bite-sized toasts as instructed below and serve with any one of our suggested toppings, or use a favorite recipe of your own.

MINI HEART SHAPED TOASTS

3 loaves white bread
extra virgin olive oil
small heart shaped
cookie cutter

Thinly slice the bread and cut out heart shapes with the cookie cutter. Arrange the individual hearts on a baking sheet, drizzle with olive oil, and toast until golden brown. Toasts may be made up to one day in advance and stored in an airtight container at room temperature.

Makes approximately 120 small heart shaped toasts. (Quantity will vary depending on size of cookie cutter and bread loaf.)

CAVIAR TOPPING

6 tablespoons
crème fraiche
2 ounces
high quality caviar

Thinly spread crème fraiche on heart toasts and top with a small dollop of caviar. Keep covered until ready to serve.

Makes approximately 40 Caviar Toasts.

CHOPPED TOMATO AND PARMESAN TOPPING

4 large tomatoes, chopped

1 red onion, chopped

4 tablespoons olive oil

2 teaspoon fresh basil, finely chopped

4 teaspoons fresh parsley, finely chopped

1/2 cup freshly grated Parmesan cheese

salt and pepper to taste

1. In a large bowl, combine tomatoes, onion, olive oil, basil, parsley, salt and pepper.

2. Place heart toasts on baking sheet and top with tomato mixture. Sprinkle with Parmesan cheese.

3. Broil for 2-3 minutes or until Parmesan cheese has completely melted. Cool for 3-5 minutes and serve warm.

Makes approximately 40 Tomato and Parmesan Toasts.

MUSHROOM AND GOAT'S CHEESE TOPPING

10 medium sized field mushrooms, sliced

4 tablespoons butter

1 red chili, finely diced

2 shallot, finely chopped

4 cloves of garlic, crushed

sprig of fresh thyme, finely chopped

1/2 lb crumbled goat's cheese

salt and pepper to taste

1. In medium sized sauté pan, melt butter. Add shallots, chili, garlic, thyme and mushrooms. Sauté on high heat until mushrooms and shallots are soft.

2. Place heart toasts on baking sheet and top with mushroom mixture. Sprinkle with goat's cheese.

3. Broil for 2-3 minutes or until Parmesan cheese has completely melted and just started to brown. Cool for 3-5 minutes and serve warm.

Makes approximately 40 Mushroom and Goats Cheese Toasts.

somewhere i have never travelled,gladly beyond
any experience,your eyes have their silence:
in your most frail gesture are things which enclose me,
or which i cannot touch because they are too near

your slightest look easily will unclose me
though i have closed myself as fingers,
you open always petal by petal myself as Spring opens
(touching skilfully, mysteriously)her first rose

or if your wish be to close to me,i and
my life will shut very beautifully,suddenly,
as when the heart of this flower imagines
the snow carefully everywhere descending;

nothing which we are to perceive in this world equals
the power of your intense fragility:whose texture
compels me with the colour of its countries,
rendering death and forever with each breathing

(i do not know what it is about you that closes
and opens;only something in me understands
the voice of your eyes is deeper than all roses)
nobody,not even the rain, has such small hands

SOMEWHERE I HAVE NEVER TRAVELLED
e. e. cummings

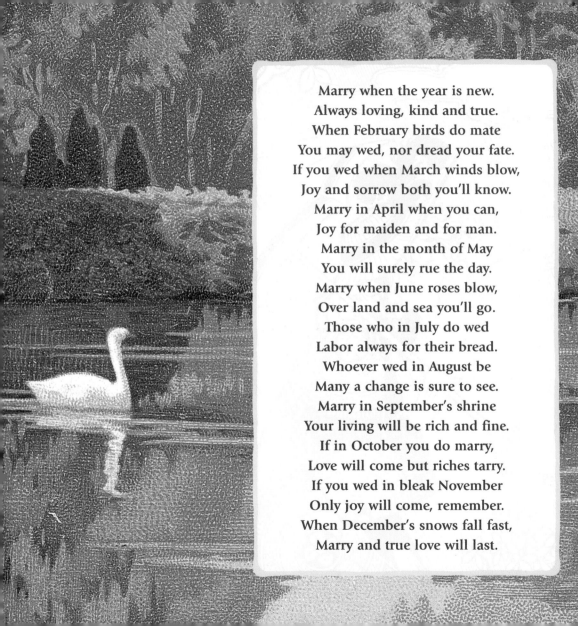

Marry when the year is new.
Always loving, kind and true.
When February birds do mate
You may wed, nor dread your fate.
If you wed when March winds blow,
Joy and sorrow both you'll know.
Marry in April when you can,
Joy for maiden and for man.
Marry in the month of May
You will surely rue the day.
Marry when June roses blow,
Over land and sea you'll go.
Those who in July do wed
Labor always for their bread.
Whoever wed in August be
Many a change is sure to see.
Marry in September's shrine
Your living will be rich and fine.
If in October you do marry,
Love will come but riches tarry.
If you wed in bleak November
Only joy will come, remember.
When December's snows fall fast,
Marry and true love will last.

Choose not alone a proper mate

Superstitions abound when it comes time for couples to choose the perfect day to wed. Chinese couples know that the first new moon of the year during peach-blossom time is extremely lucky. Others believe that to marry on the full moon is a good omen. Ancient Romans consulted numerology, and in some cases pig's entrails, to determine the best day for a wedding. In England, the groom's birthday is an exceptionally lucky day to marry; the same does not hold true for the bride's. For many, picking the right month is the first step to making sure the marriage starts off on a good note:

The ancient Greeks preferred **JANUARY**, the month dedicated to Hera, wife of Zeus. Fertility rites were common at that time of year, making it a natural time for nuptial celebrations.

FEBRUARY weddings have not always been favored among Catholics. The old English rhyme "Marry in Lent, you'll live to repent" comes from the time the Catholic Church prohibited marriages at that time of year. But according to the Celtic calendar, the first day of spring falls in February, an ideal time for couples to wed.

but a proper time to marry

Couples who marry in **MARCH** may have a belligerent relationship, like the personality of the Roman god Mars, after whom the month is named.

APRIL is ideal for lovers to tie the knot, since that month is hallowed by the Roman goddess of love, Venus.

Queen Victoria prohibited her family members to marry in the unlucky month of **MAY**. That time of year is linked to Lemuria, the Roman Feast of the Dead, during which the ancient Romans were not allowed to bathe or wear festive clothing. Not all shun May, however: It's the time of Beltaine, the Irish festival of life and fertility, when couples dance around the maypole.

The ancient Romans favored **JUNE**, still one of the most popular months to marry. Betrothed couples hoped that Juno, the goddess of women, would bring special blessings to their marriage.

In agrarian communities, people avoided marrying in **JULY** between the time of hay and harvest, to keep needed workers in the fields.

The harvest-reaping month of **AUGUST** kept many from planning wedding days, but in Ireland, it's one of the most popular times to marry. Couples who wed during the early August festival of Lughnassadh are assured of warm companionship throughout the winter months.

Many believe that marrying on the full harvest moon in **SEPTEMBER** will enhance fertility.

The Victorians cautioned, "If in **OCTOBER**, you do marry, love will come, but riches tarry." Depending upon whose advice you seek, some will say that October weddings mean a life full of work, while others insist the harvest month is a harbinger for a fertile marriage.

The ancient Greeks thought luck came to couples who wed during the colder months. An old Irish rhyme celebrates the most abundant time of year for couples to marry: "**NOVEMBER** is said time to wed, the crops is made and no warmth in bed!"

If snow falls on a **DECEMBER** wedding, the couple is sure to have a happy marriage. To marry on the last day of the year is one of the luckiest days of all, for the last memories of the year will be the couple's happiest.

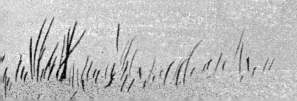

**Better to have loved a short man
than never to have loved a tall.**

DAVID CHAMBLESS

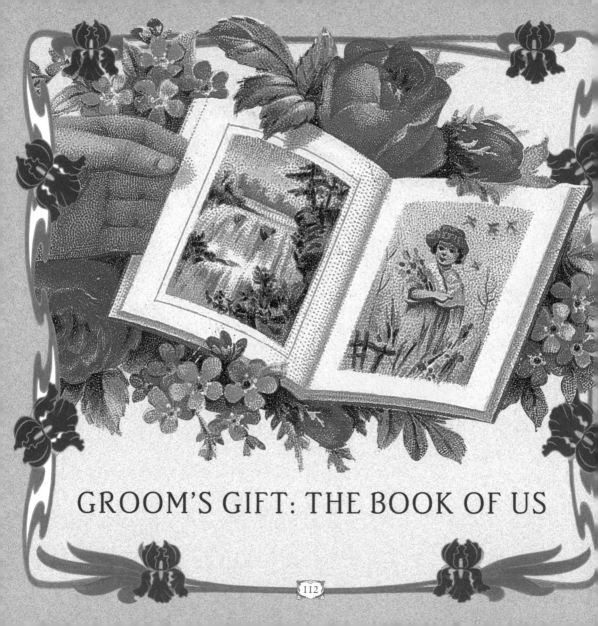

GROOM'S GIFT: THE BOOK OF US

12–24 sheets of 8 ½" x 11" lightweight card stock, 2 sheets of 9" x 11 ½" heavy-weight card stock, two pieces of 9 ½" x 11 ½" decorative fabric or leather, hole punch, scissors, craft glue, 1–2 yards of ribbon or leather cord, various colored or handmade papers, vellum or cellophane, self-adhesive photo corners

YOUR FIRST TOOTH, his first step, your bad teenage hair days, his class picture, your first date together, his first bouquet of flowers to you, your first love letter to him. You can display your early years apart and relive the romantic memories of how your lives came together in a special scrapbook that preserves the keepsakes of your past and your present, while allowing adequate space for your future. Surprise your fiancé by having it delivered to him on the morning of your wedding.

❧ Buy an album-style blank book from your local stationer or follow these simple instructions to make your own:

❧ Cut a dozen or so pages of lightweight card stock paper to the desired length and width of your scrapbook. Use a hole punch to create two or three holes along the short side of the pages.

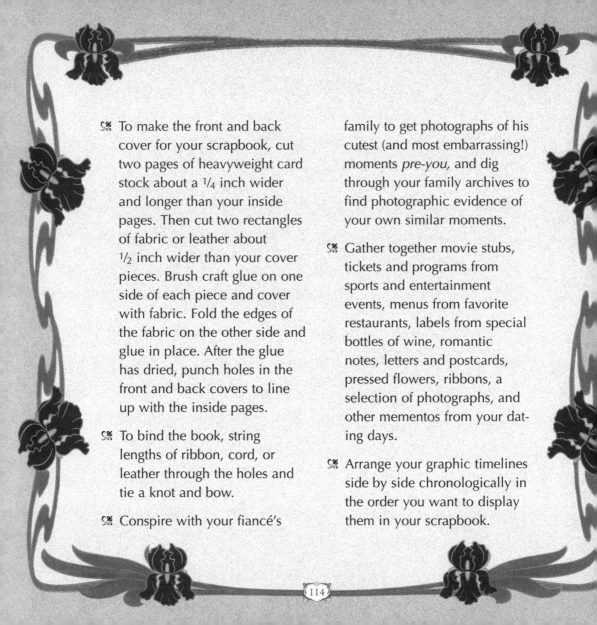

- To make the front and back cover for your scrapbook, cut two pages of heavyweight card stock about a ¼ inch wider and longer than your inside pages. Then cut two rectangles of fabric or leather about ½ inch wider than your cover pieces. Brush craft glue on one side of each piece and cover with fabric. Fold the edges of the fabric on the other side and glue in place. After the glue has dried, punch holes in the front and back covers to line up with the inside pages.

- To bind the book, string lengths of ribbon, cord, or leather through the holes and tie a knot and bow.

- Conspire with your fiancé's family to get photographs of his cutest (and most embarrassing!) moments *pre-you,* and dig through your family archives to find photographic evidence of your own similar moments.

- Gather together movie stubs, tickets and programs from sports and entertainment events, menus from favorite restaurants, labels from special bottles of wine, romantic notes, letters and postcards, pressed flowers, ribbons, a selection of photographs, and other mementos from your dating days.

- Arrange your graphic timelines side by side chronologically in the order you want to display them in your scrapbook.

- Using craft glue and old-fashioned photo corners, affix your momentos to the pages of your scrapbook. Add hand-written captions including dates and descriptions.

- To make pockets in your scrapbook for your courtship memories, cut various-sized squares of card stock. Create an aesthetic look with opaque or colored paper, handmade paper, or paper made with flower petals. Glue or sew paper squares in place along the bottom and side edges. For see-through pockets, try using vellum or heavyweight cellophane. Affix small envelopes with glue in your scrapbook to store love letters or poems. Begin the scrapbook with a private letter to your fiancé, to be read the morning of your wedding.

- If you wish to add to your scrapbook once you are married, just add pages and replace ribbons with longer pieces, if necessary.

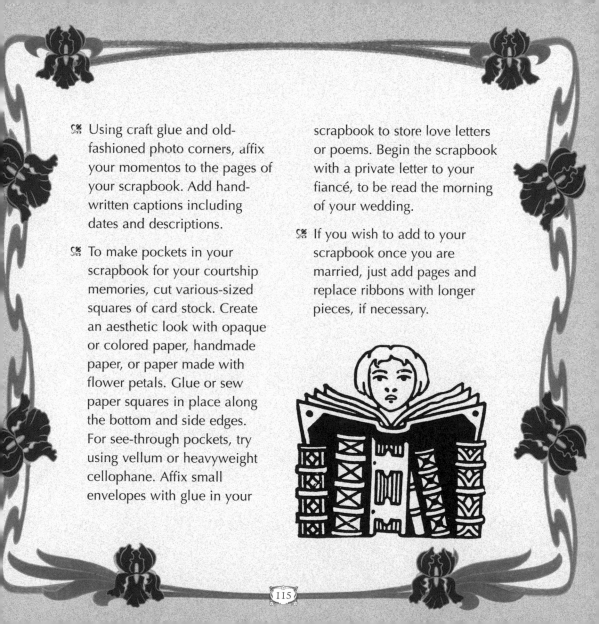

ADVICE: *Keep It Simple, Stupid*

If you're planning a wedding, the ultimate objective should be that the bride and groom have a memorable and meaningful day—the perfect beginning to their married lives together.

Anything that detracts from that objective should not be an issue. If Aunt Sally is miffed because she's seated too close to the band, she'll have to deal with it. It's not your problem.

Your objective as a married couple is to love and support one another as partners through good times and bad. "Until death" can be a long time if you're obsessing over every wrongly squeezed toothpaste tube or every visit to the in-laws. You can choose to be happily married or you can choose to be miserably married.

Families and relationships are complicated; they can be maddening. Surprises are inevitable—and they're not always going to be happy surprises. It's the tradeoff for being involved with other people, and most of us agree that the tradeoff is worth it. If you stay focused on what really matters, you'll avoid a lot of irritation. Do the simple things: Organize yourself as much as you can. Return calls promptly, pay your bills on time, and keep a list of family birthdays and anniversaries. Plan ahead, and control those areas that are within your power. Because when the unexpected occurs—and it always does—you'll be better able to cope. Keeping it simple is just a matter of eliminating all the excess baggage so you can enjoy a happier life. Trust me, you can do it. You're smarter than you look.

—FROM *KEEP IT SIMPLE, STUPID: YOU'RE SMARTER THAN YOU LOOK,*
BY JUDGE JUDY SHEINDLIN

To keep your marriage brimming,

With love in the loving cup,

Whenever you're wrong, admit it;

Whenever you're right, shut up.

Ogden Nash

*T*hanks to a love-struck Dutch maiden, modern brides are showered with gifts and surprises before they are wed. According to folklore, the custom began some three hundred years ago when the daughter of a well-to-do Dutchman fell in love with a miller. He was a good man, but her father disapproved, for the miller was poor from giving flour away to the less fortunate. When the bride's father refused to give his daughter a dowry, her friends and neighbors showered her with enough gifts and blessings so that she could marry her true love after all.

Showering the bride

Ever since, friends of brides-to-be regularly descend upon the bride and load her with advice, good luck, and presents that will start her off in her new home and new life. In the 1890s, it became fashionable to place gifts for the new bride into a Japanese parasol. Later the bride was "showered" with presents as the parasol was opened over her head. Another popular Victorian container for shower gifts was a crepe-paper wishing well.

THROUGHOUT EUROPE AND AFRICA, brides have commonly packed a trousseau, or "bottom drawer," filled with linens, clothing, and jewels. Neighbors in colonial America frequently gathered for a quilting bee, an all-day event during which they'd sew a quilt with a double wedding ring or other nuptial pattern. In Lithuania, the night before the wedding, the bride's closest friends bestow her with handwoven articles and spend the night helping her pack her hope chest. Many elder African village women will "load the bride" with words of wisdom and household goods.

SHOWERS OFTEN COME AS A SURPRISE to the bride, who can expect to be subjected to a fair amount of good-natured fun and games. Gift givers who know that each broken ribbon foretells a baby might go out of their way to wrap presents with extra ties and tape to make sure the bride will have to cut or rip them. In times past, a bridesmaid might have gathered all the ribbons into a pillow to keep in the newlyweds' home for continual good luck. Now a bridesmaid often ties all the ribbons together into a mock bouquet to use during the wedding rehearsal.

A Hurry of Showers

GREEN THUMB: An informal picnic luncheon where guests shower the bride with garden tools, seeds, bulbs, plants, and garden ornaments. Guests may also plant a bridal wreath (see page 341) for the lucky couple.

NEST BUILDER: Fill the bride's linen closets with tablecloths, lace napkins, napkin holders, towels, place mats, bed sheets, duvet covers, pillows, and pillowcases.

AROUND THE WORLD: Each guest is assigned a country and then brings a gift reflecting that culture. For example, Italy might buy a pasta maker or pizza stone; Japan, a wok or cookbook; and England, a set of teacups and fine teas.

'ROUND THE CLOCK: Assign each guest a time of day on the invitation and inform them that the gift they choose should correspond to that time—7 A.M. could be an alarm clock or bathroom accessories; 10 A.M. might be a coffeemaker or coffee mugs; lunchtime, cooking utensils or a salad bowl; bedtime, lingerie or linens, etc.

EVENING OF BEAUTY & BLISS: Guests bring candles, beauty products, spa certificates, and even classic movies for an evening of soothing music, soft aromatic candlelight, and spa fare—designed to help the bride feel relaxed, pampered, and beautiful.

RECIPE ROUND-UP: A potluck lunch or dinner where each guest brings a special dish, its recipe, and a gift to help stock the bride's kitchen. Include a blank recipe card with the invitation then collect the filled-in cards into a recipe box at the shower.

As a young girl growing up in Cleveland, Ohio, I was especially enchanted by Grandmother Barkin's most cherished possession, a quilt she had made with swatches from the wedding gowns of generations of brides in our family.

When company would come for tea, Grandmother would spread out the quilt, enthralling her guests and especially me with her tales of each delicate piece and the bride who wore it. The well-to-do brides in our family left behind swatches

GRANDMOTHER'S QUILT

RETOLD FROM A STORY BY ANNIE F. S. BEARD

of silk, satin, brocade, and velvet, while the pioneer brides of lesser means contributed their soft muslin and calico. A piece from Grandmother's own wedding gown was proudly displayed in the center of the quilt, where she had embroidered "Love One Another" atop the fading blue satin.

To my delight, Grandmother would often smile sweetly and say, "This wedding quilt will be yours one day, dear Mary." Since Grandmother had only sons and no daughter and I was the eldest granddaughter, the quilt would be passed down to me if I married first.

Although I was approaching twenty-five, I was more concerned with the kind of man I wanted to marry than getting married just for the sake of getting married. I sincerely doubted I would ever own the quilt until my childhood friend Leonard Wynn and I began to take the same path to work each day.

As Leonard and I would wind our way through the narrow streets leading to town, he would amuse me with his stories. However, one crisp fall day in 1861 any hope of our romance developing was dashed when he informed me he had enlisted in the Union army. When the day came to see him off at the train station, I felt as though my heart would break.

The enthusiasm and patriotic spirit of the women of Cleveland reached a zenith during the Civil War. And Grandmother Barkin and I were no exception. Freely and abundantly Grandmother sent supplies from her stores. But her crowning sacrifice was yet to be made.

Early one bright winter morning a carriage rolled up to Grandmother's door, and out of it stepped two eager young ladies who took Grandmother aside and said in whispered tones, "So you see, Mrs. Barkin, we are desperate for quilts for our soldiers." Slowly rising from her chair, the elderly lady stood and then proceeded to her wardrobe. Out came her treasured quilt, wrapped in white and fragrant with lavender. Calling to me, she said, "Mary, they need quilts at the hospital. I have no other ready-made ones. Are you willing to give this one up?"

I hesitated for only a moment, realizing that every gift added one more chance of comfort for my Leonard.

So Grandmother's quilt adorned one of the cots in the hospital and gave warmth and pleasure to many a poor sufferer, serving a purpose far greater than its maker had intended.

Grandmother and I joined the tireless group at the Cleveland hospital. One Christmas as I was passing from cot to cot distributing grapes and oranges, I watched the eager looks of the poor fellows. Having emptied my basket, I went to assist in feeding those who were unable to help themselves.

Taking a plate of jelly in my hand, I stepped to the side of one of the cots, noticing as I did that Grandmother's quilt lay upon the bed! The sight of it brought a rush of tender memories, filling my eyes with tears so that for a moment I didn't see the face upon the pillow.

Then, with a start, I saw Leonard Wynn. As I dried my eyes, I got a closer look at the white face with sunken eyes revealing the depth of his pain. "No, it can't be," I assured myself.

But the familiar voice erased all doubt. "Ah, Mary, I've been watching and waiting for you!"

Overjoyed I asked, "Why didn't you send for me?"

"I knew you would come sometime. The sight of this," he said, touching the quilt, "made me sure of it."

During the next few weeks, we rediscovered the joys of our companionship. That happiness was quickly extinguished, however, when I arrived at the hospital early one morning to find Leonard's bed occupied by another wounded soldier. A nurse informed me that Leonard had returned to his regiment. Along with Leonard, Grandmother's quilt had also vanished. And so, the Christmas of 1862 came and went, bringing with it joyous surprise only to snatch it and Grandmother's quilt away.

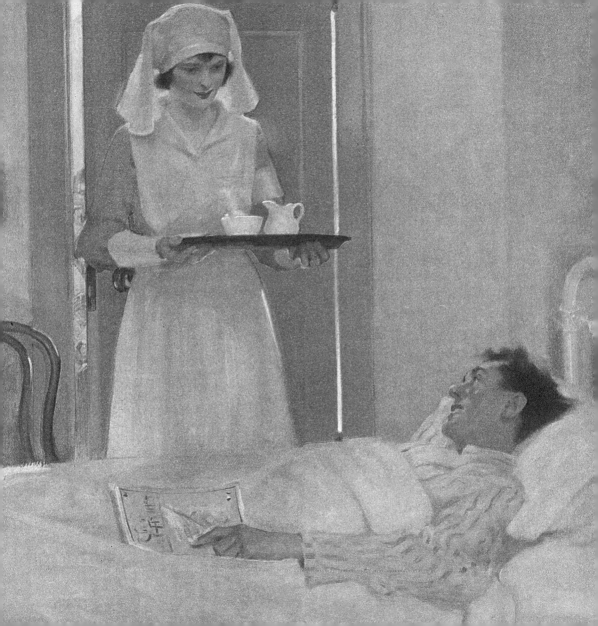

Another long year passed. I was as busy as ever, assisting the cause by trying to impart the Christmas spirit to the soldiers in the hospital. One evening at the close of the day's proceedings, I wearily laid my head down on a table. It was quickly growing dark, and I closed my eyes to snatch, if possible, a brief interval of much needed rest.

Suddenly I was startled. How long had I been asleep, and what was this lying under my head? One glance revealed Grandmother's quilt. How did it get there? I squealed with delight as I heard a familiar voice— Leonard's. "I've come for my Christmas gift, sweet Mary," he said as he drew the quilt to his chest and pointed to the inscription, "Love one another." "I wanted to ask you a year ago but decided that I would not ask you to take a maimed, sick soldier. I kept the quilt in memory of you. See, I fixed it so it would come back to you if anything happened to me." He showed me the label fastened securely to the quilt: "To be sent to Miss Mary Barkin, Cleveland, Ohio."

Then he told me how on one cold winter's day the quilt had saved his life. While sitting close to the fire to warm himself and to cook some potatoes, a stray ball from the enemy's batteries came whistling through the air, taking a straight course toward him. Luckily he was wrapped in the quilt. The ball struck him but, because of the thickness of the quilt, got no further than his coat.

That night Grandmother's quilt went back to its original owner, and my right to it as a wedding gift was firmly established by Leonard's proposal.

Had I the heavens' embroidered cloths,

Enwrought with golden and silver light,

The blue and the dim and the dark cloths

Of night and light and the half-light,

I would spread the cloths under your feet:

But I, being poor, have only my dreams;

I have spread my dreams under your feet;

Tread softly because you tread on my dreams.

HE WISHES FOR THE CLOTHS OF HEAVEN
William Butler Yeats

The best and
most beautiful
things in the
world cannot
be seen or
even touched.
They must
be felt with
the heart.

HELEN KELLER

A ROOM WITH A VIEW

E. M. FORSTER

"YOU MUST MARRY, or your life will be wasted. You have gone too far to retreat. I have no time for the tenderness, and the comradeship, and the poetry, and the things that really matter, and *for which* you marry. I know that, with George, you will find them and that you love him. Then be his wife. He is already part of you. Though you fly to Greece, and never see him again, or forget his very name, George will work in your thoughts till you die. It isn't possible to love and to part. You will wish that it was. You can transmute love, ignore it, muddle it, but you can never pull it out of you...love is eternal....

"I only wish poets would say this, too: love is of the body; not the body but of the body. Ah! the misery that would be saved if we confessed that!...When I think what life is, and how seldom love is answered by love— Marry him; it is one of the moments for which the world was made....

*O*n your wedding day, beauty and flowers will surround you. Your dearest friends and relatives, your personal "ladies in waiting," will lavish their attention upon you alone. If you're having a traditional wedding, you'll probably deck your bridesmaids out in matching gowns that complement the style and décor of the big event. But just how did this custom of look-alike bridesmaids originate?

Always a bridesmaid, never a bride

IN THE WESTERN TRADITION, the practice of surrounding the bride with similarly dressed young women started as a defense against the bride-stealing Anglo-Saxon and Germanic marauders. The earliest bridesmaids often dressed identically to the bride, in the same color gowns—including veils—to act as decoys and confuse potential kidnappers.

WHAT OF THE GROOM'S BEST MAN? In days of yore, he was generally the right-hand man of the thieving tribesman, ready to assist in snatching the unsuspecting "bride elect." Additional comrades ensured a successful raid for the groom and, if they were lucky, might steal a bride of their own.

IT WAS ALSO ONCE BELIEVED that surrounding the bride with a flock of bridesmaids would ward off harmful spirits who might place a curse on the bride and groom's happiness. Early Greek maidens often wed at age fifteen, and tradition called for these young brides to be escorted by a train of happily married, fertile women who served the dual purpose of protecting the bride from evil and allowing their own good fortune to rub off on her.

IN SOME CASES, bridal parties took extreme measures, dressing like men to protect themselves against misfortune. In Denmark, the bride and groom changed sex roles to ensure a successful wedding. One ancient Jewish tradition called for the bride to be clad in full armor, complete with helmet and weaponry.

FLORAL ADORNMENTS

A SIMPLE FLOWER can put the perfect finishing touch on any member of your bridal party. In addition to complementing the color scheme of your wedding, flowers add romantic symbolism to the event and elegance to those who wear them. You may decide to adorn junior bridesmaids or flower girls with wreaths of white rosebuds for innocence, or groomsmen with boutonnieres of evergreen berries for longevity.

HEAD WREATH

Measuring tape, florist's wire,
florist's tape, wire cutters,
flowers and foliage of choice,
assorted ribbons

1. Measure the circumference of the wearer's head and cut a piece of florist's wire about two inches longer. Make a wire hoop by overlapping the wire ends by a 1/2 inch and wrapping them together with florist's tape.

2. Trim the fresh flower and greenery stems, leaving about two inches of stem below each bloom or leaf. Bundle

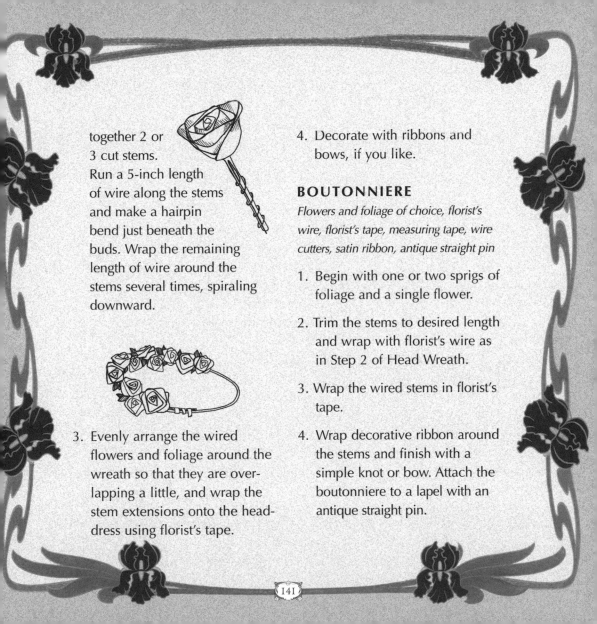

together 2 or 3 cut stems. Run a 5-inch length of wire along the stems and make a hairpin bend just beneath the buds. Wrap the remaining length of wire around the stems several times, spiraling downward.

3. Evenly arrange the wired flowers and foliage around the wreath so that they are over-lapping a little, and wrap the stem extensions onto the head-dress using florist's tape.

4. Decorate with ribbons and bows, if you like.

BOUTONNIERE
Flowers and foliage of choice, florist's wire, florist's tape, measuring tape, wire cutters, satin ribbon, antique straight pin

1. Begin with one or two sprigs of foliage and a single flower.

2. Trim the stems to desired length and wrap with florist's wire as in Step 2 of Head Wreath.

3. Wrap the wired stems in florist's tape.

4. Wrap decorative ribbon around the stems and finish with a simple knot or bow. Attach the boutonniere to a lapel with an antique straight pin.

BRIDAL TEA PARTY

In the busy days before your wedding, hosting a "girls only" bridesmaids' luncheon can be a welcome break for you and your attendants. Such occasions are ideal opportunities to thank your bridesmaids with individual gifts and an appetizing array of food. The menu for a bridal tea includes finger sandwiches and salads, most of which can be prepared a day ahead. In addition to an assortment of teas, you may want to offer sherry or champagne cocktails.

A mismatched tea set is a charming option for an informal luncheon, and if you plan to serve several different kinds of tea, you'll be using different pots anyway! Rifle through antique shops, flea markets, thrift stores, and sales at home and department stores for a variety of pretty, quality teapots, teacups, and saucers with no cracks. After lunch, wash and pack all the cups and saucers (don't forget to have some newspaper or tissue paper handy) and present each bridesmaid with one as a souvenir.

MENU SUGGESTIONS

TEA SERVICE

assorted loose black and herbal teas
cinnamon sticks
lemon and orange slices
honey
sugar cubes
cream and milk

To make the perfect pot of tea, start with cold, freshly drawn water. Bring water to a rolling boil and immediately pour a small amount in the teapot. Swirl the hot water around to warm the teapot, then discard. Place one teaspoon of tea leaves per cup of water into the teapot, then pour the water over the leaves. Steep for 3 to 5 minutes. Pour tea through a small strainer to serve.

FINGER SANDWICHES

cucumber & cream cheese
tomato & herbed butter
salmon, cream cheese, & dill
watercress & cream cheese
thinly sliced turkey & Dijon mustard-cranberry sauce spread
prosciutto & melon slices
aged cheddar & tomato

Remove the crusts from an assortment of light and dark slices of bread. Spread with herbed butter or cream cheese and various toppings. Then halve or quarter the slices to make bite-size tea sandwiches.

SWEET TREATS

fresh fruit salad
shortbread
currant scones
lemon poundcake
petit fours

A proper high tea always includes something sweet to balance the savory. If you include breakfast breads, be sure to offer butter and strawberry jam.

CHARM CAKE

Treat your attendants to a sweet slice of fortune with their tea and bake a Victorian-style bridesmaids' cake embedded with silver charms attached to long ribbons. According to lore, the bride should sift the flour with her own hands to infuse the cake with her good luck. Before the cake is cut, each bridesmaid pulls a ribbon to discover what future her charm predicts. Shop local yard sales and jewelry stores for inexpensive silver charms.

Typical Charms and Their Meanings:

airplane = travel	knot = steadfast love
anchor = life of stability	money tree = life of riches
baby buggy = children	ring = next engaged
clover = good luck	rocking chair = long life
flowers = blossoming love	telephone = good news
heart = true love will find you	wishing well = granted wish
key = happy home	wreath = contented life

FOR CAKE:

1 stick (1/2 cup) butter
1 1/4 cups sugar
1 cup milk
1 tablespoon vanilla
2 1/4 cups pastry flour
2 1/2 teaspoons baking powder
1/4 teaspoon salt
4 egg whites

1. Preheat oven to 375° F.

2. In large bowl, cream butter and sugar until light and fluffy. Add milk and vanilla and mixed until blended.

3. In separate bowl, sift flour, baking powder, and salt. Add to wet mixture in thirds. After each addition, stir the batter until smooth.

4. Whip egg whites until stiff. Fold into batter.

5. Pour batter evenly into two greased 9-inch round cake pans. Bake for about 25 minutes or until tester comes out clean. Allow to cool completely on racks before frosting.

FOR ICING:

1 stick (1/2 cup) unsalted butter
3 1/2 cups confectioner's sugar
3 tablespoons whipping cream
1 lemon rind, grated
1/2 teaspoon orange extract

1. In medium bowl, cream butter and sugar together until smooth.

2. Beat in whipping cream.

3. Add lemon rind and orange extract and mix until blended.

4. With a spatula, spread icing on top of first layer of cake. Stack second layer on top and spread remaining icing over sides of cake.

5. Arrange charms evenly around the top layer of cake. Gently press charms into the cake with your fingertip. Then carefully ice the top of the cake, leaving ribbons exposed.

Tip: To prevent ribbons from getting iced while you work, wrap them in plastic wrap or aluminum foil. Remove the wrap prior to serving.

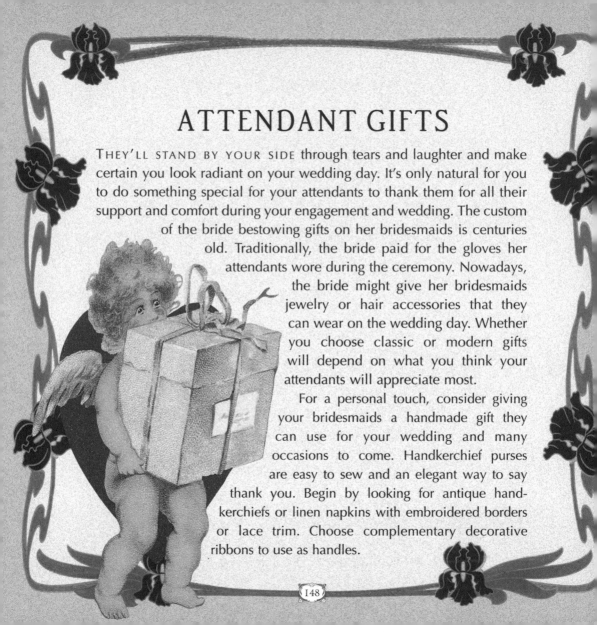

ATTENDANT GIFTS

THEY'LL STAND BY YOUR SIDE through tears and laughter and make certain you look radiant on your wedding day. It's only natural for you to do something special for your attendants to thank them for all their support and comfort during your engagement and wedding. The custom of the bride bestowing gifts on her bridesmaids is centuries old. Traditionally, the bride paid for the gloves her attendants wore during the ceremony. Nowadays, the bride might give her bridesmaids jewelry or hair accessories that they can wear on the wedding day. Whether you choose classic or modern gifts will depend on what you think your attendants will appreciate most.

For a personal touch, consider giving your bridesmaids a handmade gift they can use for your wedding and many occasions to come. Handkerchief purses are easy to sew and an elegant way to say thank you. Begin by looking for antique handkerchiefs or linen napkins with embroidered borders or lace trim. Choose complementary decorative ribbons to use as handles.

HANDMADE HANDKERCHIEF PURSE

Antique handkerchief or linen napkin, thread, pins, 18-inch length of satin ribbon

1. Starch and press handkerchief.

2. Lay handkerchief wrong side down and fold the bottom half up to meet the top edge. Pin the sides together.

3. Sew the sides by machine or by hand with a backstitch.

4. Pin ribbon ends to the inside seams and sew in place.

5. Turn the bag inside out and press.

If time is running out or you're just not the crafty type, here are some attendant gift suggestions that are both personal and readily available at most department and specialty stores:

ENGRAVED SILVER MIRRORS, COMPACTS, OR PICTURE FRAMES ❧ EARRINGS TO WEAR AT THE WEDDING ❧ SPA GIFT CERTIFICATES ❧ CRYSTAL BUD VASES ❧ LEATHER JOURNALS OR PHOTO ALBUMS ❧ SILK SCARVES ❧ PERFUME ATOMIZERS ❧ LINGERIE ❧ FOUNTAIN PENS ❧ TICKETS TO THE THEATER, A CONCERT, OR A SPORTING EVENT

Go seek her out all courteously,
And say I come,
Wind of spices whose song is ever
Epithalamium.
O hurry over the dark lands
And run upon the sea
For seas and land shall not divide us
My love and me.

Now, wind, of your good courtesy
I pray you go,
And come into her little garden
And sing at her window;
Singing: The bridal wind is blowing
For Love is at his noon;
And soon will your true love be with you,
Soon, O soon.

POEM XIII FROM *CHAMBER MUSIC*
James Joyce

*O*n her wedding day, the bride leaves behind her old life, ready to embark upon her new status as a married woman. To bridge that transition, cultures throughout the world partake in cleansing and beautifying rituals that start the bride off on the right foot. Many such customs are performed with the aid of married women, with the belief that their good fortune will rub off on the new bride.

Preparing the bride for her walk down the aisle

BODY ART

As part of several days of premarital preparation, Moroccan and Egyptian women immerse themselves in specially prepared milk baths and have body hair removed with a homemade lemon-sugar depilatory recipe. They, as well as Muslim women in India, Nigeria, and Ethiopia, are treated to full-body massages with coconut or olive oil. Finally, professional henna artists paint their hands and feet with elaborate designs. The artwork lasts for several days and is believed to keep malevolent spirits at bay.

In other parts of the world, brides have their faces adorned to greet their new husbands. Korean women have red dots painted on their cheeks and foreheads. Masai women decorate their faces and hair with red ocher dye. And in Indonesia, brides are beautified with patterns of white dots on their cheeks, noses, and foreheads.

RITUAL BATH

In China, the day before her wedding, a bride takes a purifying herbal bath prepared with bamboo, pine, and the pungent herb artemisia, so that her married life may be long, prosperous, and strong. Young Jewish women partake in a special bath called a mikvah, in which the elder women of the community participate. The bride to be is immersed several times in a special pool or natural body of water and recites a blessing for spiritual purification. She emerges from the water "born anew" to cross the sacred threshold into marriage. Navaho women also come together to prepare the bride with a ritual bath and help her dress for her nuptials. A Hopi mother will wash her daughter's hair with yucca root to purify her on her wedding day.

FOOD OF LOVE

While American brides typically lose weight in preparation for their wedding day, some brides in Nigeria, Togo, and Tanzania spend weeks eating specially made foods to fatten up so they may be voluptuous, fertile, and beautiful for their new husbands.

"**A**h, my good girrrl," cries Rabbi Lustig as he embraces me outside the synagogue after the Sabbath service. He forgets I'm no longer a child, but a young woman about to be married. He pinches my cheek as he's done every Sabbath and holiday for as long as I can remember and leaves behind the scarlet imprint of his thumb and index finger.

"*Gut Shabbas…Shabat shalom*, by good girrrl!"

There is something in the way Rabbi Lustig rolls his r's that gives me a fat, joyful feeling inside. And he never calls me by my given name. I've always been his good girrrl and nothing else.

THE MIKVAH
BY TESSA DRATT

Rabbi Lustig is tall and stout, with a thick salt-and-pepper beard that smells faintly of cigar smoke and spice. His English is imperfect, and his sermons are sprinkled with grammatical errors and turns of phrase too freely translated from another language, but I always listen to his sermons because of those wonderful rolling r's and his great, powerful voice, which, if God were to have a human voice, is surely what God's voice would sound like.

Thirty-five or so years ago, in Paris, fresh out of rabbinical school, a very young Rabbi Lustig married my mother to my father. Two weeks from now, on the East Side of New York City, he'll perform the marriage ceremony for Henry and me. Tonight, after *Shabbas* is over, Henry and I will go to the rabbi's house, a customary visit designed to show the respect due the spiritual leader of the congregation, as well as to discuss the actual logistics of the religious portion of our wedding.

The study smells of cigar smoke and old newspaper. It's dimly lit by a crooked table lamp, and piles of papers fill every available space, with the exception of the two visitor's chairs that face the cluttered desk. Henry and I sit down. Curled into a tight circle on the rabbi's own cracked-leather desk chair lie three tiny kittens, all tangled together and sound asleep. Rabbi Lustig scoops them up with one big hand as if they were three drops of water, and takes a seat in his chair, setting the kittens down again carefully in his lap.

"So…" he begins, clearing his throat and smiling. Both of his hands are occupied. With his left hand, he strokes the kittens; with his right hand, he strokes his beard.

"So…" he repeats. Henry and I look at him attentively. We've never done this before, so we sit there, across from Rabbi Lustig, and wait.

"Ah, my good girrrl, and you Henry, my young man, there is much to discuss.…begin with the easy parts."

Rabbi Lustig lays out the order of events which comprise the ceremony, then pulls out a copy of the *ketubah*, the actual marriage contract. He abandons his beard for a moment, sets his half glasses on the tip of his nose, and translates for us from the ancient Aramaic, word by word, making certain that we understand the marriage vows we are soon to take in accordance with Jewish law.

Much of this is familiar to me. I've grown up in an observant environment. Henry's lost. He's an ethnic Jew, not a religious one, and until the advent of me, Henry has managed to stay out of synagogues except for an occasional high holiday service in the fall, and that would be to please his grandparents. I glance over at him, and give him a little nudge with the tip of my shoe, but Henry's eyes are glued to the ancient and incomprehensible lettering on the strange document on the rabbi's desk. It occurs to me that Henry may be realizing for the first time just what he's about to let himself in for.

Apparently satisfied with this first portion of our meeting, Rabbi Lustig reaches across his desk and pulls a fat cigar out of the engraved humidor sitting in the right-hand corner. It seems to take forever for the rabbi to stop fiddling with the cigar and actually light the thing, but once he does, once he takes in that first long stream of smoke, holds it inside his mouth for a moment, then expels it slowly through his lips, I feel a sort of pleasure-by-association. The rabbi, Henry, and I all exhale simultaneously.

"Now…" says Rabbi Lustig from behind a blue cloud, "now, my good girrrl, now to the harder parts."

The rabbi knows, he tells me, that while I am a good Jewish girl and come to *shul* every Sabbath and every holiday with my family, he's aware that I'm also a modern young woman. I feel the blush rising from my chest to my neck to my cheeks. What does he mean? How does he know? What does he know?

"I can only tell you what is expected of you as a Jewish wife. The rest is up to you."

My eyes shoot over to Henry, for contact, for support, for something, but Henry is hopeless, staring off into smoke-filled space.

"I have made an appointment for you at the *mikvah* for next week," Rabbi Lustig says, then draws heavily on his cigar.

Probably in response to the look of horror on my face, the rabbi rather quickly exhales another blue stream of smoke and continues.

"The *mikvah* is on the West Side, near your house. It's clean and up-to-date and private. You won't mind it, you'll see. And, my good girrrl, you do understand that as an orthodox rabbi, I can't, in good conscience, perform the marriage ceremony unless you have fulfilled this particular one of your many obligations as a Jewish woman and wife...."

Henry looks directly at me for the first time since we've been in the rabbi's study. He hasn't the faintest ideas of what Rabbi Lustig is talking about. What's a *mikvah*? I read in his eyes. What the hell is a *mikvah*? Seeing the confusion on Henry's young face, Rabbi Lustig smiles and absently fondles his cigar, turning it round and round between his right thumb and index finger. Then he explains to Henry that the *mikvah* is the ritual bath that every married woman must visit once a month, after menstruation, to cleanse and purify herself according to God's laws.

A young woman's first official visit to the *mikvah* takes place before she marries—in that tiny window of time between the end of her menstrual cycle and the actual wedding day. It's a special visit, overseen by wise and pious members of the Jewish community, requiring personal preparation, purification, and benedictions.

As the rabbi talks, my attention strays. I recall my visit years ago to the communal baths in Israel, in the Old City. My stomach turns when I remember the groups of fat, flabby women sitting naked in a wide pool, bellies hanging, legs outstretched as they talk and gossip and exchange stories. The women I see before me are bald or wear kerchiefs on their shaved heads, as extremely devout Jewish matrons shave their heads in order not to attract other men with the beauty of their hair.

Henry's looking sick. I'm feeling queasy. The smell of cigar smoke in the close room is suddenly overwhelming.

"I will never ask you, my good girrrl, whether or not you have gone to the *mikvah*. I will marry you and your young man in two weeks as planned. For the rest, I count on you to do what's right."

On the appointed day, I take the Broadway bus downtown, then walk the few blocks to the inconspicuous brownstone that houses the *mikvah*. It's a brownstone like any other on the street, and only the slip of paper in my hand allows me to identify the right place. While I don't relish this process in the least, after years of having been Rabbi Lustig's good girrrl, there is little I wouldn't do out of respect for him.

I ring the bell downstairs and am buzzed into a small, dim foyer at the foot of a steep staircase. I wait.

"Come up, come up, vad are you vaiting?" calls an astringent voice from the head of the stairs.

I peer up the gloomy staircase and see a plain woman with a kerchief on her head in a white blouse, print skirt, and white bib apron. She doesn't smile, just motions me up and along and after her down a corridor. There's a faint odor of chlorine in the air. We stop in front of a metal door.

"Nu? Vat are you vaiting? Go."

I'm instructed to undress, bathe, wash my hair, remove finger- or toenail polish, cut nails, comb hair, and let her know when I'm ready by ringing a little bell I'm told I'll find in the room.

I open the metal door with trepidation, but the room inside is sparkling, and tiled in bright pink. There's a tub, a sink, a mirror, a vanity with soap, scissors, comb, and nailbrush—a fully equipped private bathing and dressing room. This room opens into an adjacent one, and I immediately peek around the corner. Amazing. The adjacent room is larger, with a tub like a miniature swimming pool or jaccuzzi in the center. There are multicolored tiles on the floor and ceiling, with steps and a handrail leading down into the center.

"Nu? I don't hear water running?" calls the woman's voice through the metal door.

I check for hidden cameras, but find none. I can only assume the aproned woman is standing directly outside the door, listening. I start a bath, undress, remove my nail polish, cut my nails, clean and wash every square inch of my body.

"I'm ready," I call through the door and ring the bell at the same time for good measure.

"Go by the pool and get in," commands the woman through the door.

Naked, pale, and thoroughly unnerved by such total exposure, I pass from one room to the other and lower myself into the square pool. I've always been a little wary of water, so I hold onto the handrail for support. The pool is heated to room temperature, and I feel more secure now that I'm covered up to my neck in warmth. A door opens, and the woman with the kerchief comes in. She shuts the door behind her. She asks:

"Do you know the *b'ruchas?*"

"No," I tell her, "I don't."

"Then you'll repeat the blessings after me." The woman recites snatches of Hebrew, a little at a time, and I dutifully repeat the phrases after her. There are many blessings. Many amens. After each amen, I'm instructed to submerge myself entirely under water. Each time I pop up, I distinctly hear men's voices chanting outside the room.

"Who's outside?" I ask.

"The *Hasidim*," the woman answers. "It's special because you're a bride. There are extra prayers....prayers the pious ones say for you...."

The dunking and repeating and praying and mumbling and chanting take about half an hour. I've simmered so long, my skin is pink and puckered.

The kerchiefed woman wipes her hands on her apron and says:

"Nu, vat you vaiting? Go. Dress. It's finished. And..."

She looks at me for a moment, sober faced as ever. I hurry back to the little dressing room and hear the woman call out softly to my retreating back.

"*Mazel tov!* Congratulations!"

"*Mazel tov, Mazel tov*," repeats a chorus of muffled male voices from somewhere behind the door.

I rush to dry off and dress and leave the premises. Excitement shoots through my body. My heart beats in my ears. In ten days' time, when Henry and I stand together under the white wedding canopy and exchange our marriage vows, when we listen to Rabbi Lustig bless our union, I will still be Rabbi Lustig's good girrrl. And never before have I felt so profoundly, exquisitely clean.

THE PAMPERED BRIDE

On her wedding day, a bride deserves to look and feel like a queen. Treat yourself to an at-home spa in the days leading up to your wedding to bring out your most beautiful self. Try these easy steps to overnight radiance.

- Soak away pre-wedding tension with a bath of Epsom salts and lavender. Add 3 cups of Epsom salts and 1 cup finely ground lavender buds to a bath of warm water. Exfoliate with a body brush and finish off by massaging coconut oil into your skin for ultimate softness.

- Revive fatigued and sensitive skin with rose water. Boil a white rose and gently rub the petals into your face until the moisture vaporizes. Or, treat yourself to a facial by mixing 2 tablespoons rose water, 2 tablespoons yogurt, 1 tablespoon honey, and 2 tablespoons dried rose petals and lavender, crumbled. Dab the mixture onto your face and relax. After 20 minutes, rinse and pat dry.

- Make your lips even more kissable with a soft-bristled toothbrush. Gently brush your lips to rub away dry or dead skin and leave them ever so smooth.

Soothe your dry eyes with the cooling properties of cucumber. A few hydrating slices on your eyes really do help hide delicate lines. When tears of joy leave your eyes red and puffy, calm them with moistened chamomile tea bags.

Give yourself shiny, voluminous hair with a protein-packed egg and avocado conditioner. Mix one egg and half of an avocado and massage into hair and scalp. Leave in for at least 20 minutes before rinsing.

Your overworked hands deserve some special attention for the moment your groom places your wedding band on your finger. Blend 1 tablespoon honey, 1 tablespoon almond oil, and $3/4$ teaspoon lemon juice. Rub the mixture into your skin and rest for

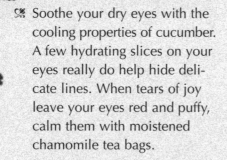

STRESS-FREE EMERGENCY PACK
Avoid last-minute mishaps by preparing a basket in the bridal suite for you and your bridesmaids. Include:
ASPIRIN ❦ BAND-AIDS ❦ CHALK OR WHITE MEDICAL TAPE (FOR HIDING SMUDGES ON WHITE FABRIC) ❦ CLEAR NAIL POLISH (FOR SNAGGED HOSIERY) ❦ COMPACT POWDER ❦ EMERY BOARD ❦ GUM OR MINTS ❦ HAIRBRUSH ❦ HAIR SPRAY ❦ LIPSTICK OR LIP BALM ❦ LOTION ❦ NEEDLE & THREAD ❦ NOTEPAD & PEN ❦ SAFETY PINS ❦ TISSUES

about 10 minutes. Rinse with warm water for soft, sweet-smelling skin.

❧ You'll be standing on them all day long, so give your feet some extra love before you walk down the aisle. Make a heel-to-toe softening foot scrub by mixing 2 cups sea salt, 2 tablespoons dried, chopped orange peel, 3 drops essential oil of lavender, and 3 drops essential oil of tea tree. Gently massage into your feet during a bath or shower.

Love is enough: though the World be a-waning,
And the woods have no voice but the voice of complaining,
Though the sky be too dark for dim eyes to discover
The gold-cups and daisies fair blooming thereunder,
Though the hills be held shadows, and the sea a dark wonder
And this day draw a veil over all deeds passed over,
Yet their hands shall not tremble, their feet shall not falter;
The void shall not weary, the fear shall not alter
These lips and these eyes of the loved and the lover.

LOVE IS ENOUGH
William Morris

Marry when the sun doth shine

Once you spread the news that you're getting married, most everyone will have a bit of advice about what ensures good luck on the Big Day. If you find a spider on your wedding gown, you'll come into money. If you marry on the incoming tide, you'll have prosperity. If you see a flock of birds, your marriage will be blessed with fertility. If it snows, you'll be wealthy. If the sun is out, you'll be a happy bride. These tried-and-true Old Wives' tales may help you garner all the luck possible on your wedding day.

DO

- 🌿 Marry under a waxing moon so happiness will grow.

- 🌿 Marry as the hands of the clock move up (after the half hour) for good fortune.

- 🌿 Throw away all the pins from your bridal wear after the wedding for a long marriage.

and you'll be a happy bride

DON'T

- 🌿 Wear the complete wedding attire before the wedding day.

- 🌿 Look in the mirror before walking down the aisle, lest you leave any part of yourself behind.

- 🌿 Allow the groom to see you in your dress before the wedding. It's bad luck to see the future before it happens.

- 🌿 Drop the ring during the ceremony, or else it's best to start over.

- 🌿 Wear the wedding ring before the wedding day.

- 🌿 Shed tears before the kiss. To cry on your wedding day prevents tears during the marriage.

- 🌿 Invite an even number of guests to attend the ceremony.

- 🌿 Feed a cat out of your wedding shoe for good luck.

- 🌿 Kiss a chimney sweep if you see one on your wedding day. You'll have good luck throughout your marriage.

- 🌿 Sew a penny into the seam of your wedding dress for luck on your wedding day and prosperity in your wedded life.

Marry in gray,
you will go far away.
Married in black,
you will wish yourself back.
Married in brown,
you will live out of town.
Married in red,
you will wish yourself dead.
Married in pearl,
you will live in a whirl.
Married in green,
ashamed to be seen.
Married in yellow,
ashamed of your fellow.
Married in blue,
he will always be true.
Married in pink,
your spirits will sink.
Married in white
you have chosen alright.

*A*ll eyes will be upon you on your wedding day. What you wear will be part of the treasured moments captured in everyone's memories for years to come. But did you know that the flowing white wedding gown is a relatively modern convention from nineteenth-century England?

Married in white

Before Victorian times, women wore their "Sunday best" dresses, which were generally light blue, lilac, rose, or pale yellow. Many brides would simply sew on additional trim or lace to make their dresses more special. Whatever the shade, the superstitious bride adhered to the custom of putting the last stitches in her gown just before walking down the aisle. This ensured that her happiness, like her gown, could not be complete until she married. Brides in other parts of the world still wear color, and lots of it:

Spanish Roman Catholic brides have traditionally worn wedding attire of **BLACK** silk with a matching lace mantilla. The gown is dedicated to an image of the Virgin Mary after the wedding.

GREEN, considered by many brides to be an unlucky color, is a favorite choice for Norwegian brides.

Nepalese and Indian brides wear **GOLD**-threaded saris on their wedding days.

you have chosen all right

The traditional colors woven into the Native American bride's dress indicate the four directions of the Earth—**BLACK** for north, **BLUE** for south, **WHITE** for east, and **YELLOW** for west.

In China and Japan, **RED** has long been a traditional color of good luck, vitality, and life. Chinese brides wear ornate gowns embroidered with golden Phoenixes. Instead of veils, they wear elaborate head-dresses made of kingfisher feathers, pearls, and gilded silver. The number of layers in the kimono worn by Japanese brides indicates her class. Royalty wear as many as twelve layers, whereas commoners wear only three. Traditionally, a Japanese bride wears an obi or dagger in her sash. She'll also wear a white headpiece to hide "the horns of jealousy" that all women supposedly possess.

Bulgarian brides still favor the traditional aladza dress, often passed down from gener-ation to generation. The dress is hand woven of wool or silk in a pattern of dark red stripes on a **RED**, **WHITE**, **YELLOW**, or **SKY BLUE** background, depending on the season. Opening like a coat, it is worn over a tunic-shaped smock of handwoven white cotton cloth finished in lace along the hem and sleeves. The bride wears a decorative apron of silk or wool in shades of red and green, with wide lace trim.

BLUE—the ancient color of purity, love, and fidelity—is popular with Irish, Amish, and Jewish brides. For her first wedding, Mary, Queen of Scots, wore a spectacular dark blue velvet gown decorated with jewels and white embroidery.

Nigerian brides don themselves in bright, **FESTIVE COLORS** and bold geometric patterns.

The New Tradition

When Queen Victoria married Prince Albert in 1839, her wedding attire set a new standard for western bridalwear for the more than 150 years since. She chose a dress made of rich white satin trimmed with orange blossoms. Her satin-and-lace train measured 18 feet. Upon her head she wore a wreath of orange blossoms and myrtle topped with a veil of fine Honiton lace. Thereafter, white gowns, floral wreaths, trains, and veils have epitomized the look of the traditional bride.

From an article originally published in Real Simple *magazine, 2001:*

I never intended to get married in a bona fide wedding dress. My plan was to walk down the aisle in red. Or black. A hip city chick, I viewed poufy white dresses as silly and demeaning—as leftovers from the Eisenhower Administration—the couture of future homemakers and Cinderella wanna-bes. Besides, why would I want to dress up like a giant fairy princess for the most adult commitment of my life?

POWER POUF
by SUSAN JANE GILMAN

Smart mouth that I am, I also felt compelled to rebel against the ever insipid "bride culture." From virtually the day I got engaged, bridal magazines—or "wedding porn," as I dubbed them—started appearing in my mailbox. Each one was loaded with 600 pages of advertisements designed to get me hot and drooling over flatware, disposable cameras, and big, confectionery dresses. "The napkins that you choose for your wedding reception," their articles intoned, "will be the most important napkins of your life…." Well, I was having none of that, thank you.

But truth be told, I also rejected the idea of wearing a traditional wedding gown because I simply couldn't bear the humiliation of shopping for one. I couldn't bear to spend hours trying on dresses that were supposed to make every woman beautiful but that would, undoubtedly, confirm that I was fundamentally, chromosomally *yech*.

My insecurity embarrassed me—as did the fact that, on some level, I was still harboring an ideal imposed on me by Walt Disney. But I found I was not the only modern woman with a few old-fashioned impulses lingering in her psyche. When I told my good, progressive friends about my plan to be the "anti-Bride," they were apoplectic. "Oh no!" they cried. "But you'll never get to wear a wedding dress again in your life!"

Just try one on, they pleaded. Just one.

Somehow, they wore me down. And irony of ironies, when I dragged myself to David's Bridal, grumbling and pessimistic, I had the most liberating shopping experience of my life.

Despite all its traditional connotations, David's Bridal is a strangely feminist place. It's a froufrou heaven staffed by women who are dedicated to making sure that other women look like goddesses.

In the dressing room, women of all colors, shapes, and sizes were deferred to, waited on, tailored to, and endorsed. I saw redheads who weighed 300 pounds and skinny black girls. Asian brides with bad dye jobs, teenagers freckled with acne, and reedy, middle-aged women who were saying, "So what if it's my third marriage? This time I'm doing it right."

And every single one of these women was made to look royally beautiful, no matter what her budget or waistline. Unlike more upscale (i.e., snooty) bridal salons, David's is one of those chain warehouses that sell dresses off-the-rack, which makes it fabulously democratic: With gowns stocked in sizes 2 to 26, it truly has something for every body.

I chose the simplest sheath dresses I could find, and they all looked terrible on me. But the saleswoman—God bless her—handled it delicately. "*Hmm*," she said. "Let's try something different just for variety's sake, OK?"

She stuck me in a big, poufy white dress—a dress with a sparkly lace train big enough to carpet a legion hall—the exact type of dress that I swore on a stack of *Ms.* magazines that I would never, ever wear.

It looked spectacular.

Then she stuck a tiara on my head. And she had me stand on a pedestal—a real live pedestal. And I looked beautiful. More beautiful than I had ever seen myself look. So beautiful, in fact, that I couldn't breathe. So beautiful that I refused to let her take me out of the dress. So beautiful that I had a total ideological and emotional meltdown right there in the dressing room.

After two hours of gaping at myself catatonically in the mirror, I finally did what every smart, modern woman does: I got out my cell phone and started frantically calling my friends. "They put me on a pedestal, and then they put a tiara on my head!" I cried. "And now I want to stay this way!"

What can I say? I loved every minute of it, and I hated myself for loving every minute of it. But as I stood there, something else became clear: Every woman should have this experience. Every woman is entitled to this. Every woman should get to see herself looking uniquely breathtaking, so that she is better equipped to withstand the ideals of our narrow-minded, narrow-waisted culture.

It was enough to make me want to take every woman I know—from my insecure teenage cousin to my self-critical boss—straight to David's Bridal for a little body worship, marital status be damned...

Only at a generic bridal warehouse did I finally feel celebrated and endorsed. Yes, they have a size 22. Yes, they have all price ranges. Yes, they will alter it for you. Yes, they will make you look beautiful. For you—*you*, my dear—are a goddess.

*F*rom head to toe, virtually every accessory the bride wears on her wedding day is rife with superstition. Here are some age-old ways women have secured their good luck on the way to the altar:

Something old, something new, something borrowed

WHEN A BRIDE wears something old, such as an heirloom, it's a link to her family roots. Something new is a show of optimism about what is to come. The good fortune of a happily married woman is sure to rub off on a new bride when she wears borrowed jewels or accessories.

THE COLOR BLUE is a symbol of purity and fidelit according to the Old Testament. Ancient Israelites we among the first to wear blue on wedding days.

TO WEAR A VEIL is certain to shield the bride from the Evil Eye. Many African brides have their hair braided to be worn as a veil.

GREEK BRIDES tuck a sugar cube inside a glove to ensure sweetness throughout marriage.

COLONIAL BRIDES carried a small pouch with a coin, a breadcrumb, wood, and cloth to be sure they'd always have money, food, shelter, and clothing.

SWEDISH BRIDES leave their shoes unfastened during their wedding ceremonies in the hopes that childbirth will come easily.

omething blue and a silver sixpence in your shoe

TO MAKE SURE they'll never be without happiness or wealth, brides throughout Europe and America slip a coin in their shoes.

A LUCKY HORSESHOE strewn with ribbons is a favored totem of Irish brides.

ADVICE: *We Know in Part*

My dear Karen,

One of the greatest things ever written on love is 1 Corinthians 13. The next time you read it, notice that the only repetition in the entire chapter is this:

"We know in part!"

The writer seems to be saying, "Back up and have one more look at the endless vistas of love. Here is something you must consider again. Beauty in human relations does not require total knowledge all at once."

We can be everlastingly thankful for this in many ways. For one thing, am I ever glad people can't see all the way through me! Then, when we go back and review it again, isn't it also fine that we don't know all about other people? If it weren't for this double protection we'd probably all join in that crazy chorus, "Stop the world, I want to get off!"

But when it applies to marriage, this is nothing less than a stupendous gift. To be married to someone in whom you see islands to be discovered, mountains to climb, valleys to explore, and new wonders beckoning off in the distance—this is absolutely the greatest.

It does create some problems though. You can't learn how to handle people such as

this all at once. It's true the days will never grow dull if you once begin this journey. Yet, on the other hand, it may also be exasperating sometimes.

So when you feel like saying, "Men! Why does my husband do such crazy things? Will I ever understand what makes him act like that?"—when you feel this way, you just be grateful for a man you can't comprehend all at once.

This beauty of a partial knowledge is what makes life with your loved ones so fascinating. It could exhaust you if you let it. But it can also keep your heart singing with the thrill of just being alive.

Your mother and I have been married twenty-six years, and—this is the truth—new thrills come fresh from her soul every day. I'm still finding out things about her I never knew before—still thankful for someone so tremendous it will take me a lifetime to search her out fully—still glad of heart the whole day long that "we know in part."

Yours for joy in the vast unknown,

Dad

—FROM *LETTERS TO KAREN*, BY CHARLIE W. SHEDD

I do not love you as if you were salt-rose, topaz,
or arrow of carnations that propogate fire:
I love you as certain dark things are loved,
secretly, between the shadows and the soul.

I love you as the plant that doesn't bloom
and carries within itself the light of those flowers,
and thanks to your love, darkly in my body
lives the dense fragrance that rises from the earth.

I love you without knowing how, or when, or from where,
I love you simply, without problems or pride:
I love you in this way because I don't know another way of loving.

but this, in which there is no you, or
so intimate that your hand on my chest is my hand,
so intimate that when I fall asleep it is your eyes that close.

SONNET XVII
Pablo Neruda

As symbols of beauty and fertility, bridal bouquets have been a central part of wedding ceremonies for centuries. In early England, the bride was thought to be imbued with the power to transmit good fortune. Hoping for a little luck, spectators tore away bits of her clothing and grabbed for her fortuitous flowers, ribbons, and headdress. In self-defense, the bride often tossed her bouquet!

A bundle of flowers

Perfumed bouquets have warded off sickness as well as provided homage to the sweetness of marriage, while aromatic nosegays of garlic, herbs, and grains were thought to keep evil spirits at bay.

No matter what kind of wedding you have, you can celebrate the floral bouquet tradition and choose from an abundance of meaningful flowers and arrangements:

ARM BOUQUET: a long, gently curved arrangement of flowers, designed to be cradled in the arm

CASCADE: a handheld bouquet that spills down from its base like a waterfall

NOSEGAY OR POSIE: a circular cluster of upright flowers held by a small handle at its base

POMANDER: a ball of densely packed, sweet-smelling herbs and flowers held by a loop of ribbon

TUSSIE-MUSSIE: a small, spiral posie with fragrant flowers and herbs, usually chosen for their meanings

WHEN YOU SELECT THE FLOWERS FOR YOUR BOUQUETS, you may want to choose varieties for their hidden meanings as well as for their outward beauty. Here's a sampling of the secret language of flowers:

AMARANTH— unfading love

AMARYLLIS— splendid beauty

APPLE BLOSSOM— good fortune

AZALEA— romance

BACHELOR'S BUTTON— hope, love

BLUEBELL— kindness

CLOVER— faithfulness

DAFFODILS AND DAISIES— sunny disposition

EVERGREEN— undying love

FIG— longevity

FORGET-ME-NOT— true love

GARDENIA— joy

HYACINTH— constancy

HYDRANGEA— devotion

IVY— fidelity

JASMINE— sensuality

LILY OF THE VALLEY— purity

MARIGOLDS— sensual passion

MINT— fecundity, virtue

MYRTLE— love, peace, happiness

ORANGE BLOSSOMS— happiness, fertility, everlasting luck

ORCHIDS— beauty, passion

PERIWINKLE— sweet memories

PHLOX— united hearts

PINE— compassion, longevity

POMEGRANATE— fertility

ROSE— love

ROSEMARY— remembrance

SAGE— domestic virtue

THYME— courage

Orange Blossoms

The evergreen orange tree blooms in all seasons, making it a natural choice as a bridal flower. According to Greek myth, Jupiter gave orange blossoms to the goddess Juno on their wedding night, while Gaea, goddess of earth and fertility, presented Hera with a garland of orange blossoms to bless her marriage to Zeus. Legend has it that this first bridal flower made its way to Europe from Saracens by way of the Crusaders. The Spanish have since laid claim to being the first to wear the orange blossom for weddings. Apparently, the daughter of a Spanish king's gardener sold a cutting from an orange tree to a French ambassador in order to earn money for her dowry. The young woman was so grateful to the tree that she wore orange blossoms in her hair on her wedding day as a tribute. The ambassador later presented the cutting to the king of France, who had it planted in his royal garden. The tree that grew is believed to be alive and well at Versailles today.

When Queen Victoria considered what to wear as a crown on her wedding day, she chose a wreath of orange blossoms rather than one of her elaborate jeweled tiaras.

PRESERVING YOUR BOUQUET

PRESERVE YOUR BRIDAL BLOOMS and keep them as a beautiful reminder of your wedding day. Here are some easy ways to make your bouquet last a lifetime.

DRIED BOUQUETS

The simple method for drying flowers is to hang them upside down in a warm, dry room. Keep them out of direct sunlight to minimize fading. They should dry in two to three weeks.

For dried bouquets that will keep their color, place the flowers on a bed of silica gel crystals in an airtight container and carefully arrange the crystals over the flowers until no air gaps are present. Seal container. Remove the crystals as soon as the flowers are dried, in about two days.

PRESSED FLOWERS

Press individual flowers between the pages of a large book and stack several heavy books on top. Allow a few weeks for the flowers to dry. You can display them in an album or frame them along with ribbons from your bouquet.

POTPOURRI

Remove all the petals from your bouquet, spread them out on a flat surface in the sun and leave them to dry for about a week. Transfer petals to a mixing bowl, add a few drops of your favorite scented oil, and toss to evenly distribute. Use your bridal potpourri to make sachets for your fine garment drawers or simply display it in a decorative bowl for all to enjoy.

THE IMPORTANCE OF BEING ERNEST

By Oscar Wilde

Oscar Wilde's play The Importance of Being Ernest *tells a humorous story of love under false pretenses. Set in late nineteenth century England, the story has friends Jack and Algernon weaving a web of lies to win the hearts of their true loves, Gwendolyn and Cecily. In the following scene, Algernon, pretending to be Jack's brother Ernest, asks for Cecily's hand in marriage.*

ALGERNON: I hope, Cecily, I shall not offend you if I state quite frankly and openly that you seem to me to be in every way the visible personification of absolute perfection.

CECILY: I think your frankness does you great credit, Ernest. If you will allow me, I will copy your remarks into my diary. (*Goes over to table and begins writing in diary.*)

ALGERNON: Do you really keep a diary? I'd give anything to look at it. May I?

CECILY: Oh no. (*Puts her hand over it.*) You see, it is simply a very young girl's record of her own thoughts and impressions, and consequently meant for publication. When it appears in volume form I hope you will order a copy. But pray, Ernest, don't stop. I delight in taking down from dictation. I have reached "absolute perfection." You can go on. I am quite ready for more.

ALGERNON (*somewhat taken aback*): Ahem! Ahem!

CECILY: Oh, don't cough, Ernest. When one is dictating one should speak fluently and not cough. Besides, I don't know how to spell a cough. (*Writes as* ALGERNON *speaks.*)

ALGERNON (*speaking very rapidly*): Cecily, ever since I first looked upon your wonderful and incomparable beauty, I have dared to love you wildly, passionately, devotedly, hopelessly.

CECILY: I don't think that you should tell me that you love me wildly, passionately, devotedly, hopelessly. Hopelessly doesn't seem to make much sense, does it?

ALGERNON: Cecily!

[*Enter* MERRIMAN.]

MERRIMAN: The dog-cart is waiting, sir.

ALGERNON: Tell it to come round next week, at the same hour.

MERRIMAN (*looks at* CECILY, *who makes no sign*): Yes, sir.

[MERRIMAN *retires.*]

CECILY: Uncle Jack would be very much annoyed if he knew you were staying on till next week, at the same hour.

ALGERNON: Oh, I don't care about Jack. I don't care for anybody in the whole world but you. I love you, Cecily. You will marry me, won't you?

CECILY: You silly boy! Of course. Why, we have been engaged for the last three months.

ALGERNON: For the last three months?

CECILY: Yes, it will be exactly three months on Thursday.

ALGERNON: But how did we become engaged?

CECILY: Well, ever since dear Uncle Jack first confessed to us that he had a younger brother who was very wicked and bad, you, of course, have formed the chief topic of conversation between myself and Miss Prism. And, of course, a man who is much talked about is always very attractive. One feels there must be something in him, after all. I dare say it was foolish of me, but I fell in love with you, Ernest.

ALGERNON: Darling. And when was the engagement actually settled?

CECILY: On the 14th of February last. Worn out by your entire ignorance of my existence, I determined to end the matter one way or the other, and after a long struggle with myself I accepted you under this dear old tree here. The next day I bought this little ring in your name, and this is the little bangle with the true lover's knot I promised you always to wear.

ALGERNON: Did I give you this? It's very pretty, isn't it?

CECILY: Yes, you've wonderfully good taste, Ernest. It's the excuse I've always given for your leading such a bad life. And this is the box in which I keep all your dear letters. (*Kneels at table, opens box, and produces letters tied up with blue ribbon.*)

ALGERNON: My letters! But, my own sweet Cecily, I have never written you any letters.

CECILY: You need hardly remind me of that, Ernest. I remember only too well that I was forced to write your letters for you. I wrote always three times a week, and sometimes oftener.

ALGERNON: Oh, do let me read them, Cecily?

CECILY: Oh, I couldn't possibly. They would make you far too conceited. (*Replaces box.*) The three you wrote me after I had broken off the engagement are so beautiful, and so badly spelled, that even now I can hardly read them without crying a little.

ALGERNON: But was our engagement ever broken off?

CECILY: Of course it was. On the 22nd of last March. You can see the entry if you like. (*Shows diary.*) "Today I broke off my engagement with Ernest. I feel it is better to do so. The weather still continues charming."

ALGERNON: But why on earth did you break if off? What had I done? I had done nothing at all. Cecily, I am very much hurt indeed to hear you broke it off. Particularly when the weather was so charming.

CECILY: It would hardly have been a really serious engagement if it hadn't been broken off at least once. But I forgave you before the week was out.

ALGERNON (*crossing to her, and kneeling*): What a perfect angel you are, Cecily.

CECILY: You dear romantic boy. (*He kisses her, she puts her fingers through his hair.*) I hope your hair curls naturally, does it?

ALGERNON: Yes, darling, with a little help from others.

CECILY: I am so glad.

ALGERNON: You'll never break off our engagement again, Cecily?

CECILY: I don't think I could break if off now that I have actually met you. Besides, of course, there is the question of your name.

ALGERNON: Yes, of course. (*Nervously.*)

CECILY: You must not laugh at me, darling, but it had always been a girlish dream of mine to love some one whose name was Ernest.

[ALGERNON *rises,* CECILY *also.*]

There is something in that name that seems to inspire absolute confidence. I pity any poor married woman whose husband is not called Ernest.

ALGERNON: But, my dear child, do you mean to say you could not love me if I had some other name?

CECILY: But what name?

ALGERNON: Oh, any name you like—Algernon—for instance...

CECILY: But I don't like the name of Algernon.

ALGERNON: Well, my own dear, sweet, loving little darling, I really can't see why you should object to the name of Algernon. It is not at all a bad name. In fact, it is rather an aristocratic name. Half of the chaps who get into the Bankruptcy Court are called Algernon. But seriously, Cecily—(*moving to her*)—if my name was Algy, couldn't you love me?

CECILY (*rising*): I might respect you, Ernest, I might admire your character, but I fear that I should not be able to give you my undivided attention.

ALGERNON: Ahem! Cecily! (*Picking up hat.*) Your Rector here is, I suppose, thoroughly experienced in the practice of all the rites and ceremonials of the Church?

CECILY: Oh, yes. Dr. Chasuble is a most learned man. He has never written a single book, so you can imagine how much he knows.

ALGERNON: I must see him at once on a most important christening—I mean on most important business.

CECILY: Oh!

ALGERNON: I shan't be away more than half an hour.

CECILY: Considering that we have been engaged since February the 14th, and that I only met you today for the first time, I think it is rather hard that you should leave me for so long a period as half an hour. Couldn't you make it twenty minutes?

ALGERNON: I'll be back in no time. (*Kisses her and rushes down the garden.*)

CECILY: What an impetuous boy he is! I like his hair so much. I must enter his proposal in my diary.

Queen Victoria's journal entries beginning on her wedding day to Albert:

10 February 1840

Got up at ¼ to 9—well, and having slept well; and breakfasted at ½ p. 9. Mamma came before and brought me a Nosegay of orange flowers. My dearest kindest Lehzen gave me a dear little ring…Had my hair dressed and the wreath of orange flowers put on. Saw Albert for the last time alone, as my Bridegroom.

JOURNAL

by QUEEN VICTORIA

Saw Uncle, and Ernest whom dearest Albert brought up. At ½ p. 12 I set off, dearest Albert having gone before. I wore a white satin gown with a very deep flounce of Honiton lace, Imitation of old. I wore my Turkish diamond necklace and earrings, and Albert's beautiful sapphire brooch….The Ceremony was very imposing, and fine and simple, and I think ought to make an everlasting impression on every one who promises at the Altar to keep what he or she promises. Dearest Albert repeated everything very distinctly. I felt so happy when the ring was put on, and by Albert. As soon as the Service was over, the Procession returned as it came, with the exception that my beloved Albert led me out. The applause was very great, in the Colour Court as we came through; Lord Melbourne, good man, was very much affected during the Ceremony and at the applause…I then returned to Buckingham Palace alone with Albert; they cheered us really most warmly and heartily; the crowd was immense; and the Hall at Buckingham Palace was full of people; they cheered us again and again…I went and sat on the sofa in my dressing-room with

Albert; and we talked together there from 10 m. to 2 till 20 m. p. 2. Then we went downstairs where all the Company was assembled and went into the dining-room—dearest Albert leading me in…Talked to all after the breakfast, and to Lord Melbourne, whose fine coat I praised.

I went upstairs and undressed and put on a white silk gown trimmed with swansdown, and a bonnet with orange flowers. Albert went downstairs and undressed.

As soon as we arrived [at Windsor] we went to our rooms; my large dressing room is our sitting room; the 3 little blue rooms are his…After looking about our rooms for a little while, I went and changed my gown, and then came back to his small sitting room where dearest Albert was sitting and playing; he had put on his windsor coat; he took me on his knee, and kissed me and was so dear and kind. We had our dinner in our sitting room; but I had such a sick headache that I could eat nothing, and was obliged to lie down in the middle blue room for the remainder of the

evening, on the sofa, but, ill or not, I never, never spent such an evening… He called me names of tenderness, I have never yet heard used to me before—was bliss beyond belief! Oh! this was the happiest day of my life!—May God help me to do my duty as I ought and be worthy of such blessings.

11 February 1840

When day dawned (for we did not sleep much) and I beheld that beautiful angelic face by my side, it was more than I can express! He does look so beautiful in his shirt only, with his beautiful throat seen. We got up at ¼ p. 8. When I had laced I went to dearest Albert's room, and we break-fasted together. He had a black velvet jacket on, without any neckcloth on, and looked more beautiful than it is possible for me to say…At 12 I walked out with my precious Angel, all alone—so delightful, on the Terrace and new Walk, arm in arm!…We talked a great deal together. We came home at one, and had luncheon soon after. Poor dear Albert felt sick and uncomfortable, and lay down in my room…He looked so dear, lying there and dozing.

12 February 1840

Already the 2nd day since our marriage; his love and gentleness is beyond everything, and to kiss that dear soft cheek, to press my lips to his, is heavenly bliss. I feel a purer more unearthly feel than I ever did. Oh! was ever woman so blessed as I am.

*M*arriage ceremonies are often abundant with scenic details such as candles, ribbons, unity symbols, and flowers. Virtually every bit of wedding décor is rich with imagery that dates back to antiquity.

Setting the scene for romance

TO SCATTER ROSE PETALS and sweet-smelling herbs on the bridal path is to wish for a future of sweetness and fertility. In days of old, wedding guests would throw grains and wheat along the path to bless the couple with a fruitful and bountiful marriage.

WHEN QUEEN VICTORIA wore a wreath of myrtle and orange blossoms, she was honoring the mythical gods of the Greeks and Romans. Aphrodite, the goddess of love, emerged from the ocean accompanied by nymphs wearing wreaths of myrtle.

FLOWERS BUNDLED with ribbons and knots harken back to times when lovers literally tied the knot to wed.

GARLANDS OF IVY represent faithfulness and strength, for these hearty vines are difficult to disturb once they've rooted.

THE FLAME FROM A CANDLE is a reminder of spiritual light, earthly fire, and good wishes for hearth and home. Ancient Romans illuminated their weddings with torches. Young Greek brides are escorted to the altar by candlelight.

COLOR HAS ALWAYS played an important role in weddings: blue for purity, red for vitality, white for innocence, green for fertility and luck.

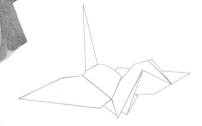

JAPANESE BRIDES traditionally fold 1001 origami cranes to decorate the wedding hall. Since cranes mate for life, the display of these good-luck birds symbolizes a thousand-fold wish for marital happiness. In Korea, butterfly motifs decorate fans, screens, clothing, and furnishings as symbols of everlasting love and beauty.

GUEST BOOK MEMORIES

ONCE THE OFFICIAL RECORD of all the witnesses at a wedding, the guest book now makes a wonderful keepsake that the bride and groom can revisit over the years to be reminded of the heartfelt wishes from friends and relatives. Instead of having your guests sign their names in a typical journal-style book, invite them to contribute wishes or personal stories that will add to a richer treasury of your wedding day. Consider these ideas:

BOWL OF WISHES

Display a large vase or glass bowl on a prominent table at your reception. Provide small note cards with envelopes and pens that encourage guests to write wishful quips or to wax poetic about you and the groom. Later you can glue the envelopes onto the pages of an empty scrapbook album where you can reopen them to read the cards inside.

PICTORIAL GUEST BOOK

This inventive guest book includes candid photos of all your guests taken at your wedding with a Polaroid camera. Prepare an empty old-fashioned photo album by affixing photo corners throughout to fit the dimensions of the Polaroid stills. Place the album alongside the camera with a small sign instructing each guest to take a picture of themselves, add it to the guest book using the pre-adhered photo corners, and write their wishes and congratulations for the bride and groom below their candid.

MEMORY CARDS

Provide cards in your wedding invitations and ask guests to describe how they met you and/or your groom. When your invitation responses come in the mail, collect all the cards, mount them in a decorative album, and display the book at your reception for others to browse through. It's sure to inspire happy memories.

Nothing is worth more than this day.

GOETHE

THE WINGS OF THE DOVE

By Henry James

Set in England in the early 20th century, The Wings of the Dove is the tragic tale of a love triangle caused by the division of the classes. When Kate falls in love with a poor journalist named Merton, she must choose between her heart and her inheritance. In this scene, she secretly promises herself to Merton.

AT THIS POINT Kate ceased to attend. He saw after a little that she had been following some thought of her own, and he had been feeling the growth of something determinant even through the extravagance of much of the pleasantry, the warm transparent irony, into which their livelier intimacy kept plunging like a confident swimmer. Suddenly she said to him with extraordinary beauty: "I engage myself to you for ever."

The beauty was in everything, and he could have separated nothing—couldn't have thought of her face as distinct from the whole joy. Yet her face had a new light. "And I pledge you—I call God to witness!—every spark of my faith; I give you every drop of my life." That was all, for the moment, but it was enough, and it was almost as quiet as if it were nothing. They were in the open air, in an alley of the Gardens; the great space, which seemed to arch just then higher and spread wider for them, threw them back into deep concentration. They moved by a common instinct to a spot, within sight, that struck them as fairly sequestered, and there, before their time together was spent, they had extorted from concentration every advance it could make them. They had exchanged vows and tokens, sealed their rich compact, solemnized, so far as breathed words and murmured sounds and lighted eyes and clasped hands could do it, their agreement to belong only, and to belong tremendously, to each other.

ADVICE: *Honor the Relationship*

To keep a marriage healthy, the first thing is to honor the relationship itself. Come to it as something led by spirit. The next step is to acknowledge each other's soul, acknowledge each other not just as human beings but as spirits who have chosen a body to come into. Then, through ritual, bring these two souls together.

Perhaps couples in the West could use meaningful things they have had since childhood, objects that have become sacred to them. With the presence of relatives or friends, bring those two sacred objects together in a pot or basket, then keep them in a space reserved as a shrine. It can be kept in the bedroom, or somewhere in the house where both can have access to it.

You can use that special place to draw energy from, especially when things become hard. You can go back to that source, access the time before problems came, and really draw energy from that.

Say Yes

People think that when they say yes once, it means yes forever. But in the indigenous context, no. That's why you have to constantly renew your vows, whether it's once a year or when somebody else is getting married.

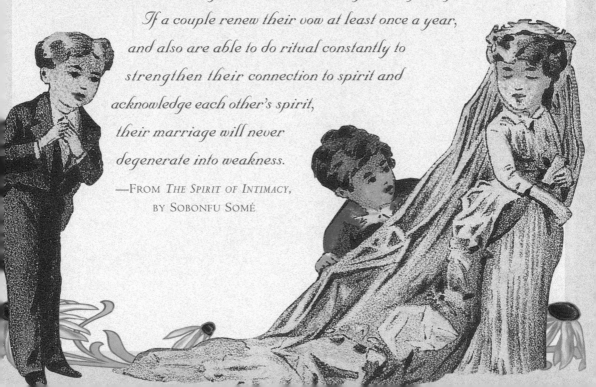

If a couple renew their vow at least once a year, and also are able to do ritual constantly to strengthen their connection to spirit and acknowledge each other's spirit, their marriage will never degenerate into weakness.

—From *The Spirit of Intimacy*,
by Sobonfu Somé

I honor your gods

I drink at your well

I bring an undefended heart to our meeting place

I have no cherished outcome

I will not negotiate by withholding

I am not subject to disappointment

CELTIC VOW

To have and to hold,

*I*t's the time everyone is waiting for: the ceremony that will unite the bride and groom as wife and husband. Traditions that have grown out of both common law and religious practices will usually include a processional, a blessing, vows, a unifying ritual such as an exchange of rings, and the nuptial kiss. How this happens is what makes each wedding unique.

In Jewish weddings, couples come together under the *chuppah*, a canopy that symbolizes the sanctuary of a new home and the spiritual haven the bride and groom will share together. Male members of the congregation hold up each corner of the chuppah during the ceremony. In days of old, traveling bridal parties protected the bride under a canopy en route to meet the groom. Anglo-Saxons held a veil or canopy

from this day forward

called a "care-cloth" over the heads of both the bride and groom while the couple exchanged vows. In China, an elder woman holds an umbrella over the bride's head during the ceremony.

Polynesian bridal couples marry under a bark cloth called a *kapa*. Today, many couples choose to exchange vows under an arbor of flowers in the hope that their marriage will continue to grow and flourish.

Russian Orthodox brides and grooms are crowned king and queen for a day. Witnesses hold silver and gold crowns above the marrying couple's heads during the course of the ceremony. Greek Orthodox couples are crowned with leaves and flowers. The priest leads the couple three times around the altar, after which the bride and groom drink from the same cup of wine to seal their commitment.

Hindu couples take the ceremonial Seven Steps, or *Saptha Padhi*, around a flame together. Each time they pass the flame they make specific promises to each other to enter into a nourishing household blessed with health, wealth, harmony, happiness, children, longevity, and life-long companionship.

Many marrying couples exchange food or drink instead of vows. In Japan and Korea, Shinto ceremonies unite the bride and groom with sake, "the drink of the gods." In a celebration of an old formal bond between two people, the bride and groom take turns drinking three sips from three different sake cups. The order and number of sips vary from village to village. Often the couple's families are invited to drink afterward. In China, couples participate in a tea ceremony. The sweet drink is often specially made with ingredients that connote double meanings, such as dried lily bulbs, or *bok hop*, which also sounds like the phrase that means "a hundred years together." In Nigeria, Yoruban bridal couples share a "tasting of the elements." Both bride and groom take a taste of lemon, vinegar, cayenne pepper, and honey to experience the sour, bitter, hot, and sweet aspects of marriage. In Burma, Buddhist couples place their hands in a bowl of water during the ceremony to symbolize the creation of a union as "indivisible as water."

Not all couples seal their marriage with a kiss. In Hawaii, the bride and groom exchange leis and rub their noses together to celebrate their nuptial bond. Most wedding ceremonies conclude with much cheering and delight. The tradition of church bells, cars honking, or horns or drums playing lives on from the days of old, when people made noise to scare away jealous spirits.

> **WHEN IS A KISS MORE THAN A KISS?** In ancient Rome, the kiss was legally binding; the public gesture between two betrothed people meant as much as an exchange of rings.

I did not stand at the altar, I stood
at the foot of the chancel steps, with my beloved,
and the minister stood on the top step
holding the open Bible. The church
was wood, painted white inside, no people—God's
stable perfectly cleaned. It was night,
Spring, outside a moat of mud,
and inside, from the rafters, flies
fell onto the open Bible, and the minister
tilted it and brushed them off. We stood
beside each other, crying slightly
with fear and awe. In truth, we had married
that first night, in bed, we had been
married by our bodies, but now we stood
in history—what our bodies had said
mouth to mouth we now said publicly,
gathered together, death. We stood
holding each other by the hand, yet I also

stood as if alone, for a moment,
just before the vow, though taken
years before, took. It was a vow
of the present and the future, and yet I felt it
to have some touch on the distant past
or the distant past on it, I felt
the silent dry crying ghost of my
parents' marriage there, somewhere
in the bright space—perhaps one of the
plummeting flies, bouncing slightly
as it hit *forsaking all others*, then brushed
away. I felt as if I had come
to claim a promise—the sweetness I'd inferred
from their sourness; and I felt as if
I had come, congenitally unworthy, to beg.
And yet, I had been working toward this love
all my life. And then it was time
to speak—he was offering me, no matter
what, his life. That is all I had to
do, there, to accept that gift
I had longed for—to say I had accepted it,
as if being asked if I breathe. Do I take?
I do. I take as he takes—we have been
practicing this. Do you bear this pleasure? I do.

THE WEDDING VOW
By Sharon Olds

WEDDING KEEPSAKE

THE EXCHANGE OF RINGS is one of the most sacred moments during the wedding ceremony. Make it more meaningful by having the ring bearer deliver your wedding bands on a pillow that you make yourself. It is destined to become a family heirloom enjoyed by generations to come. Consider these ideas for simple, elegant ring pillows:

- If you're having your dress or your bridesmaids' dresses made, save a few swatches of material about 8 inches square for your ring pillow.

- Consider sewing on charms, colors, or symbols that reflect your ethnic heritage. For example, miniature horseshoes for Irish couples, blue fabric for Jewish couples, or phoenix and dragon imagery for Chinese couples.

- Honor a beloved grandmother or great aunt by fashioning a ring pillow out of an heirloom handkerchief.

- Use craft glue to affix small pressed flower petals to the material of your ring pillow.

TO MAKE A PILLOW:

*2 pieces of 8-inch square fabric,
sewing needle, thread, pillow stuffing,
10–12 inch satin ribbon, scissors*

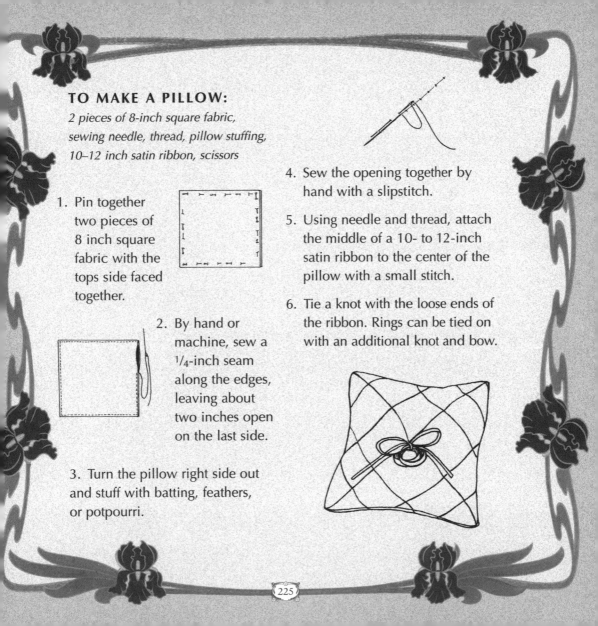

1. Pin together two pieces of 8 inch square fabric with the tops side faced together.

2. By hand or machine, sew a ¼-inch seam along the edges, leaving about two inches open on the last side.

3. Turn the pillow right side out and stuff with batting, feathers, or potpourri.

4. Sew the opening together by hand with a slipstitch.

5. Using needle and thread, attach the middle of a 10- to 12-inch satin ribbon to the center of the pillow with a small stitch.

6. Tie a knot with the loose ends of the ribbon. Rings can be tied on with an additional knot and bow.

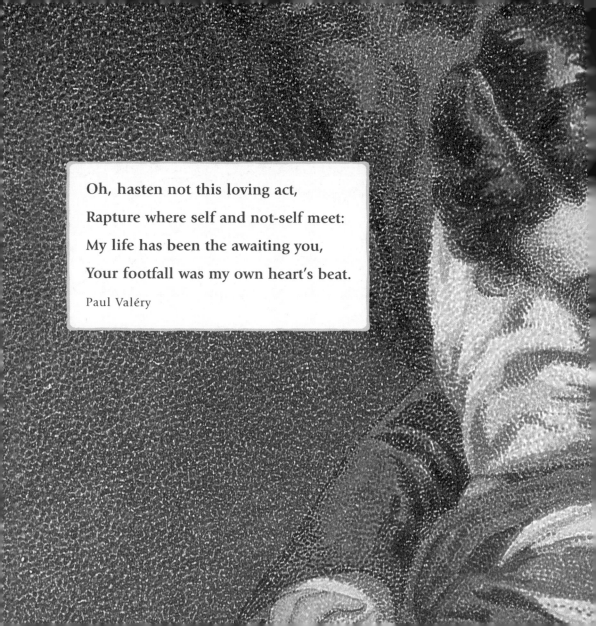

Oh, hasten not this loving act,
Rapture where self and not-self meet:
My life has been the awaiting you,
Your footfall was my own heart's beat.

Paul Valéry

THE BOOK AND THE BROTHERHOOD

BY IRIS MURDOCH

"…I HEREBY GIVE MYSELF. I love you. You are the only being whom I can love absolutely with my complete self, with all my flesh and mind and heart. You are my mate, my perfect partner, and I am yours. You must *feel* this now, as I do….It was a marvel that we ever met. It is some kind of divine luck that we are together now. We must never, never part again. We are, here in this, *necessary* beings, like gods. As we look at each other we verify, we *know*, the perfection of our love we *recognise* each other. *Here* is my life, here if need be is my death."

We have taken the seven steps. You have become mine forever. Yes, we have become partners. I have become yours. Hereafter, I cannot live without you. Do not live without me. Let us share the joys. We are word and meaning, united. You are thought and I am sound.

May the nights be honey-sweet for us; may the mornings be honey-sweet for us; may the earth be honey-sweet for us; may the heavens be honey-sweet for us.

May the plants be honey-sweet for us; may the sun be all honey for us; may the cows yield us honey-sweet milk!

As the heavens are stable, as the earth is stable, as the mountains are stable, as the whole universe is stable, so may our union be permanently settled.

FROM THE HINDU MARRIAGE RITUAL OF "SEVEN STEPS"

*W*hat will make your wedding unique? Perhaps a family custom that celebrates your cultural heritage. Or maybe a symbolic ritual to bless your marriage with children. Whether you borrow from the past or begin anew, you'll be continuing an age-old tradition of celebrating wishes of happiness, love, and fruitfulness in married life.

❦ IN KOREAN TRADITION, the groom presents his future mother-in-law with a goose, an animal which mates for life, to symbolize his fidelity to his new bride. The bride's mother shows her acceptance by offering noodles to the goose. Modern Korean grooms present wooden geese to their new in-laws, and the term "feeding noodles to the goose" remains a euphemism for getting married. Japanese couples will have a goose and gander join the wedding procession to bring good luck to their marriage.

Jumping the broom, feeding the goose

AFRICAN-AMERICAN COUPLES celebrate the beginning of their new life together by jumping the broom, a custom practiced by Southern slaves, who were unable to marry legally. The ceremony, also known as a *besom* wedding, called for the groom to lay a broom on the ground with bristles facing north. He'd then take his bride's hand and they would jump over. The bride would then turn the broom around so that the bristles faced south, take her groom's hand, and they would jump over again. A similar custom of crossing sticks was practiced throughout Africa, Wales, and rural England. In addition to warding off bad luck, the broom or sticks alluded to the vitality of trees and symbolized the beginning of wedded life.

and tying the knot

🌸 AT THE END OF A JEWISH CEREMONY, the groom crushes a glass under his foot as a remembrance of the fragility in life. The witnesses welcome the act with cheers of *Masel tov!* Some Japanese grooms will break an egg with their bare foot during the ceremony. The raw yoke symbolizes fertility.

🌸 "TYING THE KNOT" got started with the ancient Egyptians, and was also practiced by the medieval Celts. In a ceremony called handfasting, couples had their hands bound together while they pledged their fidelity. The practice is shared by Latin couples, who bind themselves together with cord, leather, or a vine. This custom survives in the Episcopal wedding ceremony, in which the minister binds the hands of the bride and groom together with his stole for part of the ceremony. In India, a marriage was considered legal and binding when the Hindu groom tied a ribbon around the neck of his bride. In ancient Carthage, a bride and groom were married by knotting their thumbs together with a leather strip. In ancient African custom, the groom would tie braided grasses around the bride's wrists and ankles.

❧ THE CUSTOM OF THROWING RICE has multiple origins. Once wedding guests would throw grains and figs at the newlyweds to wish them fertility. In Poland it was customary for onlookers to throw wheat and oats. After some noble weddings, the bride and groom would throw coins newly minted for the occasion. Modern wedding-goers throw birdseed, confetti, or flower petals, or blow bubbles over the newlyweds.

❧ IN A TRADITIONAL POLISH WEDDING, the *oczepiny*, or "capping ceremony," marks the moment when the bride becomes a married woman. The event takes place the evening of the wedding day, usually after the bride has danced with all the unmarried men. Young girls then remove the bride's wreath of rue, and married women place a cap on her head. Customarily, the bride removes the cap twice; the third time the women place it on her head, she keeps it on, joining in more singing and dancing.

Going!

Going!!

Afoot and lighthearted, take to the
   open road,
Healthy, free, the world before you,
The long brown path before you
   leading wherever you choose.

Say only to one another:
Camerado, I give you my hand!
I give you my love more precious
   than money,
I give you myself before preaching or law:

Will you give me yourself? Will you
   come travel with me?
Shall we stick by each other as long
   as we live?

SONG OF THE OPEN ROAD
Walt Whitman

ADVICE: *Travel Tips*

It occurs to me that marriage, like traveling, would be easier if one had a guidebook as well as a good companion. Since neither Michelin nor Baedeker publishes a guide to marriage, as an experienced traveler I offer a few tips for the journey.

- *Choose a mate who's physically and emotionally appealing. You don't want to wake up one morning to find you've been sleeping with the ugly grumpling.*

- *Memory lapses can be a boon to a happy marriage. You can't hold a grudge if you can't remember the problem.*

- *Training in the diplomatic corps would be useful, but if you can't afford to spend a year abroad, read how our founding fathers compromised to create the Constitution.*

- *Sign up for a Berlitz course, the language of the opposite sex. You can't communicate if you don't share a common tongue.*

🌼 Find common interests (for example, if he likes history and she likes shopping, buy shoes at Gettysburg!).

🌼 Maintain your sense of humor. This will enable you to retain your perspective and ignore the wrinkles, potbellies, balding heads, and in-laws.

If you follow these tips and travel with an amiable partner, you're not apt to lose your way. Bear in mind, though, that there are dips in the road, occasional detours, and patches of ice to confront every traveler.

Patti

—FROM *FROM THE HEART*

MADAME BOVARY

By Gustave Flaubert

Madame Bovary tells the story of Emma, a French country girl during the mid—nineteenth century who yearns for a life of passion and sophistication. Betrothed to a kind doctor named Charles, Emma has a joyous and elaborate wedding.

THE GUESTS ARRIVED EARLY, in carriages, one-horse traps, two-wheeled wagonettes, old cabs minus their hoods, or spring-vans with leather curtains. The young people from the neighboring villages came in farm-carts, standing up in rows, with their hands on the rails to prevent themselves from falling: trotting along and getting severely shaken up. Some people came from thirty miles away, from Goderville, Normanville and Cany. All the relatives on both sides had been invited. Old estrangements had been patched up and letters sent to long-forgotten acquaintances.

Every now and then the crack of a whip would be heard behind the hedge. Another moment, and the

gate opened, a trap drove in. It galloped up to the foot of the
steps, pulled up sharp and emptied its load. They tumbled out on
all sides, with a rubbing of knees and a stretching of arms. The
ladies were in bonnets, and wore town-style dresses, with gold
watch-chains, and capes with the ends tucked inside their sashes,
or little colored neckerchiefs pinned down at the back, leaving
their necks bare. The boys were dressed like their papas,
and looked uncomfortable in
their new clothes. Many,
indeed, were that day
sampling the first

pair of boots they had ever had. Beside them went a big girl of fourteen to sixteen, cousin or elder sister no doubt, all red and flustered and speechless in her white first-communion dress (let down for the occasion), with a rose pomade smarmed over her hair, and gloves that she was terrified of getting dirty. As there were not enough stablemen to unharness all the carriages, the gentlemen pulled up their sleeves and went to work themselves. According to the difference in their social status, they wore dress-coats, frock-coats, jackets or waistcoats.

The mayor's office being within a mile and a half of the farm, they made their way there on foot, and returned in the same manner after the church ceremony was over. At first the procession was compact, a single band of color billowing across the fields, all along the narrow path that wound through the green corn; but soon it lengthened out and split up into several groups, which dawdled to gossip. The fiddler led the way, his violin adorned with rosettes and streamers of ribbon. After him came the bride and bridegroom, then the relatives, then the friends, in any order; and the children kept at the back, amusing themselves by plucking the bell-flowers from among the oat-stalks, or playing among themselves without being seen. Emma's dress was too long and dragged on the ground slightly. Now and again she stopped to pull it up, and then with her gloved fingers she daintily removed the coarse grasses and thistle burrs, while Charles waited, empty-handed, until she had finished.

The wedding-feast had been laid in the cart-shed. On the table were four sirloins, six dishes of hashed chicken, some stewed veal, three legs of mutton, and in the middle a nice roast sucking-pig flanked by four pork sausages with sorrel. Flasks of brandy stood at the corners. A rich foam had frothed out round the corks of the cider-bottles. Every glass had already been filled to the brim with wine. Yellow custard stood in big dishes, shaking at the slightest jog of the table, with the initials of the newly wedded couple traced on its smooth surface in arabesques of sugared almond. For the tarts and confectioneries they had hired a pastry-cook from Yvetot. He was new to the district, and so had taken great pains with his work. At dessert he brought in with his own hands a tiered cake that made them all cry out. It started off at the base with a square of blue cardboard representing a temple with porticoes and colonnades, with stucco statuettes all round it in recesses studded with gilt-paper stars; on the second layer was a castle-keep in Savoy cake, surrounded by tiny fortifications in angelica, almonds, raisins and quarters of orange; and finally, on the uppermost platform, which was a green meadow with rocks, pools of jam and boats of nutshell, stood a little Cupid, poised on a chocolate swing whose uprights had two real rosebuds for knobs at the top.

The meal went on till dusk. When they got tired of sitting, they went for a stroll round the farm, or played a game of "corks" in the granary, after which they returned to their seats. Towards the end some of the guests were asleep and snoring. But with the coffee there was a general revival. They struck up a song, performed party-tricks, lifted weights, went "under your thumb," tried hoisting the carts up on their shoulders, joked broadly and kissed the ladies. The horses, gorged to the nostrils with oats, could hardly be got into the shafts to go home at night. They kicked and reared and broke their harness, their masters swore or laughed; and all through the night by the light of the moon there were runaway carriages galloping along country roads, plunging into ditches, careering over stone-heaps, bumping into the banks, while women leaned out of the doors trying to catch hold of the reins.

The bride had begged her father to be spared the customary pleasantries. However, a fishmonger cousin—the same who had brought a pair of soles for his wedding-present—was about to squirt some water out of his mouth through the keyhole of their room, when Roualt came up just in time to prevent him and explain that his son-in-law's position in the world forbade such improprieties. Only with reluctance did the cousin yield to that argument.

Charles had no facetious side, and hadn't shone at his wedding. He responded feebly to the puns and quips and innuendoes, the compliments and ribaldries, which it was considered necessary to let fly at him as soon as the soup appeared.

Next morning, however, he seemed a different man. He was the one you would have taken for yesterday's virgin. Whereas the bride gave nothing away. The slyest among them were nonplussed. They surveyed her as she approached with the liveliest curiosity. But Charles made no pretenses. He called her "my wife," addressed her affectionately, kept asking everyone where she was, looked for her everywhere, and frequently led her out into the yard, where he was seen, away among the trees, putting his arm round her waist, leaning over her as they walked, and burying his face in the frills of her bodice.

Two days after the wedding, husband and wife departed. Charles could not be away from his patients any longer. Roualt let them have his trap for the journey, and accompanied them himself as far as Vassonville. There he kissed his daughter for the last time, then got down and started back homewards. When he had gone about a hundred yards, he halted; and the sight of the trap going farther and farther into the distance, its wheels turning in the dust, drew from him a deep sigh. He remembered his own wedding, his early married life, his wife's first pregnancy. He had been pretty happy himself, that day he took her from her father and brought her home mounted behind him, trotting over the snow. For it had been round about Christmas-time, and the country was all white. She held on to him with one arm, her basket hung from the other; the wind lifted the long lace ribbons of her Caux headdress, so that sometimes they flapped over his mouth; and when he turned his head, he saw, close beside him against his shoulder, her rosy little face quietly smiling beneath the gold crown of her bonnet....long ago it was, all that....In his brain, still clouded with the fumes of the feast, dark thoughts and tender memories mingled.

Often the traditional wedding banquet, symbolic of the official commencement of the new marriage, is as important as the ceremony itself. No matter what time of day the nuptials take place, many refer to the celebrated feast as the "bridal breakfast" because it is the first meal the bride and groom share as husband and wife. In some African communities, a couple is not considered married until the ceremonial breaking of bread. The word *bridal* comes from the term *bride's ale*, a common English festivity that would take place in a local tavern after the ceremony. Guests would pay for their own ale to help keep the wedding costs down.

Eat, drink, and be married!

The splendid array of food at Chinese and Japanese wedding banquets is rich with symbolism and good wishes for the couple's future. Each dish, through its color and presentation, evokes thoughts of abundance, love, fertility, and prosperity. Red foods, like lobster, tuna, and pork, are eaten for luck; noodles for long life; and chestnuts for many children. Vegetables make their appearance cut into fans for a bright future, cranes for fidelity, turtles for longevity. Many dishes blend cool and hot ingredients or sweet and sour flavors to represent the balance of yin and yang in marriage.

No feast is complete without the customary toasts to bless the bride and groom. This joyful tradition may have started among the wine lovers of France. At banquets, people customarily put a small bit of bread in a goblet to soak up the sediment from the wine. Guests would pass the goblet around for everyone to take a sip. The person who got the "toast" at the end would be rewarded with good luck.

CONFECTIONARY FAVORS

In the seventh century when weddings were regularly rowdy affairs, brides tacked favors of ribbons, flowers, and lace on their dresses. Immediately after the ceremony, guests ran to the bride and pulled them off for good luck, stripping the bride of all her adornments. Nowadays, favors can range from table centerpieces to little boxes of "groom's cake" for guests to take home. Edible favors are particularly popular among guests and couples alike. Personal and easy to make, fortune cookie favors are an original way to send your guests home with messages of love.

PERSONALIZED FORTUNE COOKIES

½ cup butter
1 cup confectioner's sugar
4 egg whites
½ teaspoon vanilla extract
1 cup pastry flour

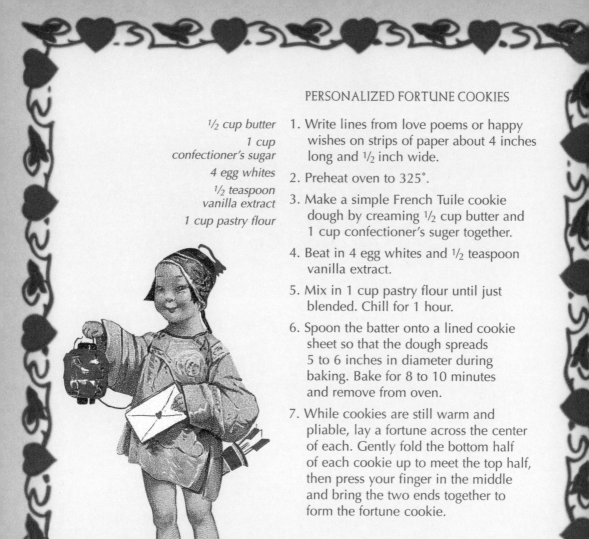

1. Write lines from love poems or happy wishes on strips of paper about 4 inches long and ½ inch wide.

2. Preheat oven to 325°.

3. Make a simple French Tuile cookie dough by creaming ½ cup butter and 1 cup confectioner's suger together.

4. Beat in 4 egg whites and ½ teaspoon vanilla extract.

5. Mix in 1 cup pastry flour until just blended. Chill for 1 hour.

6. Spoon the batter onto a lined cookie sheet so that the dough spreads 5 to 6 inches in diameter during baking. Bake for 8 to 10 minutes and remove from oven.

7. While cookies are still warm and pliable, lay a fortune across the center of each. Gently fold the bottom half of each cookie up to meet the top half, then press your finger in the middle and bring the two ends together to form the fortune cookie.

Other suggested favors that can be either handcrafted or store-bought:

Take Away Centerpieces

- A cluster of shallow dishes lined with attractive stones containing blooming paperwhites.

- A collection of small sand-filled decorative flowerpots holding elegant slender candles of various heights.

Place Card Keepsakes

- Mount decorative name placards onto poster board or foam matting, trim to size, then affix a magnet to the back of each one.

Gifts That Grow

- Wrap forget-me-not seed packets in ribbon or lace for guests to take home and plant in honor of the bride and groom.

The Gift of Music

- Create a CD containing a mix of many of the songs you plan to play during the wedding celebration.

For the Kids

- Goodie bags that hang on the back of each child's chair at the reception are sure to keep your young guests busy throughout your wedding day. Personalize simple canvas tote bags with iron-on letters spelling out each child's name. Fill the bags with colored pencils, a sketch book, activity books, jellybeans, candied almonds, a deck of playing cards, and stickers.

This marriage be wine with halvah,

  honey dissolving in milk.

This marriage be the leaves and fruit

  of a date tree.

This marriage be women laughing

  together for days on end.

This marriage, a sign for us to study.

This marriage, beauty.

This marriage, a moon in a light blue sky.

This marriage, this silence fully mixed

  with spirit.

THIS MARRIAGE
Rumi

A day that is not danced

Where there's dancing, there's joy, especially at weddings. One of the most romantic moments is when the bride and groom dance together for the first time as a married couple, swaying and gliding to what is commonly known thereafter as "their song." Once the floor opens to everyone else, the festivities really begin, with the classic celebratory dances specially reserved for weddings. Here's a small sampling:

At Cajun weddings, unmarried girls traditionally **DANCE ALONE** with a broom. But in Slovakia, the bride dances with a broom to welcome a happy home life.

Bridesmaids and single women at a Norwegian wedding will blindfold the bride for the **"CROWN DANCE,"** for a chance to wear the bride's gold-and-silver-bangled headdress. Once the music begins, the bride tries to capture one of her single friends and crown her. The dancing continues until all the participants have had the opportunity to wear the crown.

Dancing is a central part of Irish weddings, where guests compete in contests to do **THE BEST JIG**. The winner takes the cake, literally: a miniature version of the wedding cake.

is a day that is not lived

One of the most festive moments at a Jewish wedding is the celebrated *Horah*, or **CHAIR DANCE**. Guests hoist up chairs holding the bride and groom and dance to "Hava Nagila." At Irish weddings, the groom's best lads will lift the groom up in a "jaunting chair" and dance him around the room.

The **MONEY DANCE** is a favorite in Poland, the Philippines, and Hawaii. Guests must pay to dance with the bride and groom by pinning money to their clothing or placing it in special pouches worn by the bride and groom.

A French Canadian custom allows the bride and groom to poke fun at their unmarried older siblings during **THE SOCK DANCE**. The single siblings wear colorful embroidered socks and take center stage while others tease them.

Italian brides and grooms dance **THE TARANTELLA**, an exotic dance that increases with speed as it nears the end, leaving everyone breathless and exhausted!

Some Favorite First Dance Songs

"A Fine Romance," JOE DERISE

"Ain't No Mountain High Enough," ASHFORD & SIMPSON

"Ain't Nothing Like the Real Thing," ARETHA FRANKLIN

"And I Love Her," THE BEATLES

"Can't Take My Eyes Off You," LAURYN HILL

"Crazy for You," MADONNA

"From This Moment On," ELLA FITZGERALD

"Have I Told You Lately That I Love You," VAN MORRISON

"I Do," PAUL BRANDT

"I Love You," MARTINA MCBRIDE

"Is This Love," BOB MARLEY

"It Had to Be You," HARRY CONNICK JR.

"I Will Always Love You," WHITNEY HOUSTON

"Love and Happiness," AL GREEN

"Love Me Tender," ELVIS PRESLEY

"My Cherie Amour," STEVIE WONDER

"No Ordinary Love," SADE

"Someone Like You," VAN MORRISON

"Stand by My Woman," LENNY KRAVITZ

"Take My Breath Away," BERLIN

"The First Time Ever I Saw Your Face," ROBERTA FLACK

"What Is This Thing Called Love," ROSEMARY CLOONEY

"When a Man Loves a Woman," PERCY SLEDGE

"When I Fall in Love," NAT KING COLE

"Woman," JOHN LENNON

"You Send Me," ARETHA FRANKLIN

You are my [husband/wife]

My feet shall run because of you.

My feet, dance because of you.

My heart shall beat because of you.

My eyes, see because of you.

My mind, think because of you.

And I shall love because of you.

ESKIMO LOVE SONG

Love does not consist in gazing
at each other, but in looking outward
together in the same direction.

ANTOINE DE SAINT-EXUPÉRY

Next to the bride and groom in all their finery, the wedding cake is often the grandest display of the nuptial celebration. For many purists, a proper wedding cake is an elaborately decorated work of culinary art no less than three tiers high. The top tier is often saved for a first anniversary or a christening.

A little slice of happiness

ONE OF THE MOST ANTICIPATED MOMENTS of the reception is the bride and groom's partaking of their first shared responsibility as a married couple: cutting the cake. The tradition started long before the invention of cake as we know it today. Ancient Greeks crumbled small biscuits on top of the bride's head in the belief that blessing her with a symbol of good fortune from the harvest would grant her ease in childbirth. The ancient Romans made bread-cakes from grain, salt, and water to break over the bride's head in a ceremony called *confarreatio*. Guests would scramble to catch the falling crumbs for good luck.

ALTHOUGH PEOPLE IN THE MIDDLE AGES missed out on the gastronomic pleasure of fine confectionery, they did much to inspire the modern wedding cake. Biscuits soon gave way to spicier breads and buns, which guests heaped in large piles at the wedding feast. The bride and groom then shared a kiss over the buns—the kiss was said to bless them with good luck—before distributing the pastries to their guests. Bakers caught on to this custom and started icing the buns with honey to make them stick together and therefore stack more easily. These festive treats were the precursors to the modern-day "groom's cake," traditionally kept in small boxes for the guests to take home.

BY THE SIXTEENTH CENTURY, spiced plum cakes were all the rage at weddings. These dense, heavy breads were filled with dried raisins, currants, plums, and in some cases almonds. For centuries, these alcohol-preserved concoctions remained the most common style of wedding cake. It wasn't until the 1800s that the French discovered the secrets of baking powder and baking soda and developed the fine milled flours used today. *Voilà!* The contemporary wedding cake was born.

THANKS TO QUEEN VICTORIA and other royals, the craze for elaborate, multi-tiered cakes spread throughout Europe. The primary centerpiece of Queen Victoria's wedding was a plum cake that measured 3 yards in circumference and 14 inches in depth, and weighed 300 pounds! In 1923, the Viscount Lascelles and Princess Mary topped that with a royal wedding cake that stood 9 feet tall and weighed a whopping 800 pounds.

GROOM'S CAKE

In the Southern United States, the groom's cake started as a second layer of dark wedding cake on top of a larger layer of white cake. The bridal couple would cut cake from the bottom tier, and serve the dark cake on a later date. By the late 1800s, the groom's cake became a separate dessert to be divided and presented to guests in small white boxes.

In the American tradition, groom's cakes are often rich chocolate cakes, although they may be fruit or nut cakes as well. In some cases the groom's cake reflects the groom's personality; instead of being served in boxes, it will be a large sheet cake in the shape of a sailboat or football, for example. For an elegant twist on the tradition, make a tiered tower of chocolate cupcakes that can be taken home by guests as wedding favors at the end of the reception. The recipe that follows includes a sprinkling of ground almonds, an ingredient that symbolizes undying love. Each batch makes 12 cupcakes. Repeat the recipe until the number of cupcakes equals the number of guests.

CHOCOLATE CUPCAKE TOWER

4 tablespoons
cocoa powder
(preferably Dutch)

½ cup
boiling water

¾ cup sugar

1 ½ cup self-rising
cake flour

¾ cup very soft
unsalted butter

2 large eggs

1 teaspoon
vanilla extract

12-cup muffin pan
lined with paper
baking cups

1. Preheat the oven to 400°. In a stainless steel bowl, mix the cocoa to a paste with the boiling water and set aside to cool.

2. Mix the sugar and the flour. In a large bowl add the butter and ½ of the cocoa mixture. Mix well and put aside.

3. Beat the eggs, the rest of the cocoa mixture and the vanilla well. Dribble slowly into the sugar mixture, beating constantly until it is creamy.

4. Spoon into the paper baking cups in the pan and bake for 20 minutes, until a toothpick comes out clean.

5. Leave in the pan for 5 minutes, then remove the cupcakes in the paper baking cups and cool on a wire rack. Cool completely before frosting.

FROSTING & DECORATION

1 ⅓ cups confectioner's sugar, sifted

4 ounces cream cheese

3 oz. bittersweet chocolate shavings

3 oz. ground almonds

1. When the cupcakes are completely cool, make the frosting by beating together the sifted confectioner's sugar and cream cheese until soft.

2. Frost cupcakes and sprinkle with ground almonds and chocolate shavings.

3. Stack cupcakes in square layers, making a tiered tower. The size of the base layer will depend on the total number of cupcakes being used. Each ascending layer should be one less cupcake in width. For example, to make a 140-cupcake tower, here's how to stack each layer:

    1st layer: 7 cupcakes wide (49 cupcakes)

    2nd layer: 6 cupcakes wide (36 cupcakes)

    3rd layer: 5 cupcakes wide (25 cupcakes),

    4th layer: 4 cupcakes wide (16 cupcakes)

    5th layer: 3 cupcakes wide (9 cupcakes)

    6th layer: 2 cupcakes wide (4 cupcakes)

    7th layer: 1 cupcake

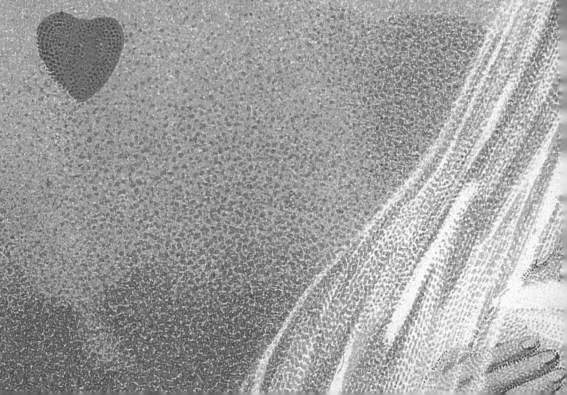

Success in marriage depends on being able, when you get over being in love, to really love.... You never know anyone until you marry them.

ELEANOR ROOSEVELT

See, when you're by yourself, you apply your own standards. It doesn't bother your Self that you stand in the middle of the room, drink 32 ounces of club soda, and belch out everything you've eaten since the Spring. Your Self may not care. Others, however, may.

And if you're with another person all the time, every repugnant component of your life must, by definition, happen in front of the other person. There's nowhere to hide.

So you learn to accept each other. Your best behavior is now and forever reserved for *outside* the house, and once you're inside, you're free to be the repellent American you really are. There's a tacit

COUPLEHOOD
BY PAUL REISER

understanding. "I know all about *you*, you know all about *me*, and it'll all be our little secret."

You become a little team. It's the "two of you" against "everybody else." And you look out for each other. Your partner becomes the one person in the world you can go over to and say, "Do I have anything in my nose?"

That's your mutual job: protect your Ugly Truths from everyone but each other. Which is kind of nice, actually. Here is someone who will not only be honest with you, but whose love for you is so great it can withstand looking up your nose. Then they go right back to loving you like it never happened.

It's ironic that Everybody Else—to whom you owe nothing—is spared having to see what's in your nose. As if *they* deserve better. But your partner, the very person you love more than all others, gets to look right in there and investigate personally. That's *their* little privilege. One of the many bonuses for signing on for the long haul.

ADVICE: *Break Some Rules*

One of the best lessons I learned about life and, indirectly, about marriage was from our two dogs. Our first was an over trained poodle who never did anything wrong. We loved him dearly, but after a while he became boring. Our second was a daffy, dizzy shorthaired pointer. She was poorly trained, barked madly at everyone, and thought she was an equal member of the family. She ruined our carpets the first week we had her, stole our food, demanded attention, and nevertheless charmed all of us with her verve and high spirits. When she was chastised, she made sure we loved her by snuggling up until we patted her generously.

The lesson: It does not pay to be good, bland, and ultimately boring. Take a risk, break some rules, get the love you need by asking for it. This will keep a marriage frisky and charm the one who most needs charming.

Rita

—FROM *FROM THE HEART*

The great secret of a
successful marriage is
to treat all disasters as
incidents and none of
the incidents as disasters.

SIR HAROLD NICOLSON

Wedding celebrations are often rife with frolicsome antics and pranksters who revel at playing tricks on the bride and groom. Many of these good-humored festivities originated from old superstitions about keeping evil spirits away or protecting the bride from thieving marauders. In any event, the fun and games allow others to wish happiness and prosperity to the newlyweds and, in some cases, garner good luck for themselves!

Merriment & mischief

IT'S CONSIDERED GOOD LUCK AT IRISH WEDDINGS when the Straw Boys arrive. The custom prevailed in the countryside, where uninvited young men, with straw stuffed in their hats and clothes to disguise their appearance, would gate-crash wedding parties, often providing music and dance entertainment. In the midst of their singing and merriment, they usually insisted upon dancing with the bride until offered food and drink. At the end of the night, the bride and groom were crowned with smaller straw hats. A symbol of fertility, straw was thought to bring good luck to the couple.

IN THE SIXTEENTH AND SEVENTEENTH CENTURIES, when most weddings were raucous affairs, guests regularly chased the bride and groom to their honeymoon chambers and invaded their room. Just about everything concerning the bride and groom was considered good luck—including their clothing. The bride would relent, throwing a stocking at the single women, who clamored to catch it and be next to wed. Today, the stocking has been replaced with a garter worn around the bride's leg.

IN THE RURAL UNITED STATES, newlyweds can expect a late-night "shivaree" from noisy friends and neighbors. The crowd serenades the couple with boisterous shouting until the husband humors them with treats. The practice is also called "belling," "collathump," and "skimmilton." In some cases the group might continue their revelry in the couple's new home, taking all the labels off the canned goods or forcing the bride and groom to do stunts. The custom comes from the medieval French *chariviari*, which means a loud display of rough music.

THE GERMAN CUSTOM OF STEALING THE BRIDE has its roots in medieval abductions. During the reception the groom's best man whisks the bride away to a bar, where they drink champagne until the groom finds them and pays their tab. In Wales, the bride and her family ride away on horseback, with members of the groom's family and his groomsmen in pursuit. Sometimes the custom ends in a raucous mock battle wherein the groomsmen "fetch the bride" for the ceremony.

GERMAN COUPLES have a lively night of feasting and frolicking on *Polterabend*. The night before the wedding, friends, neighbors, and unexpected visitors descend upon the couple for a rowdy evening. As part of the festivities, guests put on a mock play of what the bride and groom's married life will be like, and they might string baby items on the clothesline. After a night of dancing and drinking, guests will break the old china and crystal to symbolize a fresh start for the new couple. The bride and groom sweep up the shards to assure their good fortune in a happy home with many children.

Never above you.
Never below you.
Always beside you.

WALTER WINCHELL

Sometimes our life reminds me
of a forest in which there is a graceful clearing
and in that opening a house,
an orchard and garden,
comfortable shades, and flowers…
The forest is mostly dark, its ways
to be made anew day after day, the dark
richer than the light and more blessed,
provided we stay brave
enough to keep on going in…

THE COUNTRY OF MARRIAGE
Wendell Berry

That romantic moment when the groom carries his bride over the threshold isn't just a display of gallantry; it's an ancient homage to the protector of hearth and home. The virgin Roman goddess Vespa considered the threshold sacred. Ancient Roman grooms therefore carried out this symbolic gesture to avoid letting their virgin brides touch the threshold and thereby risk being disrespectful of the goddess.

Home is where the heart is

IN SOUTH AFRICA, to symbolize the fire of a new family's hearth, both sets of parents bring fire from their own homes to light the first fire in the bride and groom's new home.

THE CHIMNEY was a traditional passage-way for unwanted spirits to enter the home. Upon their initial entry, Russian couples burn straw in the hearth to smoke out any demons that might be hiding in the flue.

OTHER CULTURES feared that evil spirits lurked in the ground near the threshold, waiting to trip the bride as she entered. Some brides would toss grains of salt across the threshold to ward off malevolent spirits. The belief was that if a witch were to try and enter the newlywed's home, she would have to stop and count every grain of salt before she could come inside, and would get discouraged and leave.

MANY COUPLES christen their new homes with symbols of fidelity and fertility. French brides break an egg in the doorway to ensure healthy and happy children. Spanish brides are known to keep an olive branch in the house to make sure their husbands stay faithful. In Greece, the bride's mother meets the bride at the door of the newlyweds' home. The mother gives the new bride a drink of honey and water so that her words will always be sweet. She then uses the rest of the drink to paint the threshold, so that their home remains a place of sweetness and peace.

FENG SHUI YOUR MARRIAGE

FENG SHUI IS AN ANCIENT SYSTEM that strives to achieve harmony between people and their environment. Based on the Taoist tradition of perceiving nature as five elemental energies (*chi*), Feng Shui masters try to understand the natural order of cause and effect: why things happen to us when they do, and by extension, what we can do to steer ourselves onto a different path. Reordering *chi* in your environment can affect every aspect of your life—even your chances of a happy marriage. Here are a few tips to encourage good *chi* on your wedding day and in the marital home.

FENG SHUI YOUR WEDDING

- A bride should go to her wedding in a red car, but if that isn't possible, either a maroon, yellow, or white vehicle makes a good substitute for enhancing strong *yang* energy. An endless knot should also be tied to the front of the car, which signifies undying love between the couple.

- When the bride and groom arrive at the reception venue, they should be greeted by a loud sound, such as the band playing a rousing rendition of the wedding march—this has the double effect of representing *yang* energies while also announcing the start of the celebration.

When decorating the reception hall, make sure that there are no dried flowers anywhere, including potpourri. It's also a good idea to have all the colors of the nine lives represented somewhere within the hall—dark blue or black, red, yellow, pink, gold or purple, gray or silver, and white. This will help keep all the energies balanced, giving the couple an auspicious beginning to their marriage.

The wedding vows should be exchanged within red envelopes. The red color symbolizes strong *yang* energy, which will imbue your words with power and luck, while the rectangular shape of the envelope heralds back to the protection provided by ancient Chinese shields.

Newlyweds should follow the ancient Chinese tradition of drinking tea with their parents right after the wedding when they are still in their wedding clothes, so that they may honor their elders and receive their blessings.

FENG SHUI YOUR HOME

Before a newlywed couple moves in together, the following feng shui ritual should be performed to bring good fortune to all eight corners of their house. Mix a dash of saffron with water until it yellows, and pour a few drops on every floor in the northern end of the home, known as the water sector, to help kindle and sustain love. In the northeast and southwest areas, fill a bucket with sand from a riverbank and mix it with the ashes from three incense sticks. Scatter the sand over the corners, and wait a day before cleaning it up to activate energy in the two earth sectors of your home. In the east and southeast, the two wood areas, place seven flowers—lily, peony, chrysanthemum, plum blossom, lotus blossom, orchid, and a bulb flower. If any of these are unavailable, choose blooms from each of the four seasons to bring good fortune all year-round. In the southern fire sector, activate *yang* energy by lighting three red candles. In the west and northwest metal sectors, strengthen the *chi* with three gold or silver pieces. Walk around this sector with a dish of these in hand.

- It is bad feng shui to have the marital bed reflected in a mirror. In fact, the larger a mirror is, the more negative chi a marriage will have, because mirrors can leave couples wanting to look elsewhere for more satisfaction. While positioning mirrors directly behind the bed or covering them with a heavy drape can lessen the potential harm, it's best to remove them entirely from the bedroom.

- Light earth tones are the perfect color for your bedroom because earth energies nurture your body. Fiery colors like red and hot orange should be avoided. While they do incite the passions, they also keep you from a restful sleep. Colors like blue and purple should be kept away from the bed at all costs since they have a servile and chaste connotation.

* It is important to remove anything with pointy corners from your bedroom, such as your dresser, especially if it's at head-level. This sends out negative energy, or *shar* chi, and can cause stress and disputes between couples. Ideally, your furniture should be round and curved, which gives off good *chi* by mimicking the form of the human body.

* To promote a good relationship, try to double up when you decorate. For instance, instead of one bedside lamp, consider a pair, one for each side of the bed. Two pieces of rose quartz are particularly

auspicious in the bedroom. While the mandarin duck is thought to bring good fortune to those who have not yet found a mate, a pair of flying geese symbolizes the happiness of marriage, and helps to reinforce the fidelity of a couple.

I was wrapped in black
fur and white fur and
you undid me and then
you placed me in gold light
and then you crowned me,
while snow fell outside
the door in diagonal darts.

While a ten-inch snow
came down like stars
in small calcium fragments,
we were in our own bodies…
and you were in my body…
and at first I rubbed your
feet dry with a towel
because I was your slave
and then you called me
princess.
Princess!

Oh then
I stood up in my gold skin
and I beat down the psalms
and I beat down the clothes
and you undid the bridle
and you undid the reins
and I undid the buttons,
the bones, the confusions,
the New England postcards,
the January ten o'clock night,

and we rose up like wheat,
acre after acre of gold,
and we harvested,
we harvested.

US
Anne Sexton

*T*he last bit of cake has been eaten, the last dance done, the last farewell spoken—and at last the bride and groom are alone to let the honeymoon begin.... Not necessarily!

IN THE SIXTEENTH CENTURY, the groomsmen and bridesmaids saw to the bedding of the bride and groom. The attendants first blessed the nuptial bed by lacing it with ribbons and surrounding it with fragrant herbs before shepherding the newlyweds to their bridal chamber. They then undressed the couple and placed them in bed. Often, the attendants served the bride and groom "sack-posset," a spiced hot milk fermented with wine or ale. Pranksters might sew the sheets together or tie bells to the newlyweds' bedsprings.

IN THE IRISH COUNTRYSIDE, friends of the bridal couple bless the nuptial bed by fetching an egg-laying hen and tying it to the bedposts in hopes of procuring a fresh egg on the bride-bed. It was also hoped that some of the hen's fertility would be passed on to the couple.

The first night

IN AFRICA AND CHINA, friends of the wedding pair place a baby or fresh fruit in the bed before the bride and groom share it. After a Chinese wedding banquet, many of the guests warm up the bridal bed and cajole the newlyweds into playing erotic games, such as giving the groom wine that he must transfer to the bride's mouth or scattering beans on the bride's body for the groom to pick up with his mouth.

IN ANCIENT TIMES, fire played an important role on the honeymoon night. The Roman bride was escorted to the bridal chamber by torchlight and the torch was later thrown to the wedding guests. According to early Polish custom, a new bride's bedchamber was laden with flowers, and male guests would circle the room with burning candles to chase away demons before the groom could enter.

IT WAS CUSTOMARY in the late eighteenth and early nineteenth centuries for Irish newlyweds to take a different path home from their wedding festivities than the one they took to the wedding. This was to avoid the pranks of friends and family as well as the *sidhe*, or faeries, who were thought to be waiting to whisk the bride away and steal her fine dress.

of the rest of your life

SUPERSTITION DICTATES in many parts of the world that if the bride and groom sleep with their heads facing north (the compass point of happiness) on their wedding night, they will have happiness in their married life.

Believe it or not, the following is an excerpt from the Madison Institute Newsletter, Fall 1894:

To the sensitive young woman who has had the benefits of proper upbringing, the wedding day is, ironically, both the happiest and the most terrifying day of her life. On the positive side, there is the wedding itself, in which the bride is the central attraction in a beautiful and inspiring ceremony, symbolising her triumph in securing a male to provide for all her needs for the rest of her life. On the negative side, there is

INSTRUCTION AND ADVICE FOR THE YOUNG BRIDE

BY RUTH SMYTHERS, BELOVED WIFE OF THE REVEREND L.D. SMYTHERS

the wedding night, during which the bride must pay the piper, so to speak, by facing for the first time the terrible experience of sex.

At this point, dear reader, let me concede one shocking truth. Some young women actually anticipate the wedding night ordeal with curiosity and pleasure! Beware such an attitude! A selfish and sensual husband can easily take advantage of such a bride. One cardinal rule of marriage should never be forgotten: GIVE LITTLE, GIVE SELDOM, AND ABOVE ALL, GIVE GRUDGINGLY. Otherwise, what could have been a proper marriage could become an orgy of sexual lust.

On the other hand, the bride's terror need not be extreme. While sex is at best revolting and at worst rather painful, it has to be endured, and has been by women since the beginning of time, and is compensated for by the monogamous home and by the children produced through it. It is useless, in most cases, for the bride to prevail upon the groom to forgo the sexual initiation. While the ideal husband would be one who would approach his bride only at her request, and only for the purpose of begetting offspring, such nobility and unselfishness cannot be expected from the average man.

Most men, if not denied, would demand sex almost every day. The wise bride will permit a maximum of two brief sexual experiences weekly during the first months of the marriage. As time goes by she should make every effort to reduce this frequency.

Feigned illness, sleepiness, and headaches are among the wife's best friends in this matter. Arguments, nagging, scolding and bickering also prove very effective, if used in the late evening about an hour before the husband would normally commence his seduction.

Clever wives are ever on the alert for new and better methods of denying and discouraging the amorous overtures of the husband. A good wife should expect to have reduced sexual contacts to once a week by the end of the first year of marriage and to once a month by the end of the fifth year of marriage.

Just as she should be ever alert to keep the quantity of sex as low as possible, the wise bride will pay equal attention to limiting the kind and degree of sexual contacts. Most men are by nature rather perverted, and if given half a chance, would engage in quite a variety of the most revolting practices. These practices include amongst others performing the normal act in abnormal positions.

When he finds her, the wife should lie as still as possible. Bodily motion on her part could be interpreted as sexual excitement by the optimistic husband. If he attempts to kiss her on the lips she should turn her head slightly so that the kiss falls harmlessly on her cheek instead. If he attempts to kiss her hand, she should make a fist. If he lifts her gown and attempts to kiss her anyplace else, she should quickly pull the gown back in place, spring from the bed and announce that nature calls her to the toilet. This will generally dampen his desire to kiss in the forbidden territory.

If the husband attempts to seduce her with lascivious talk, the wise wife will suddenly remember some trivial non-sexual question to ask him. Once he answers she should keep the conversation going no matter how frivolous it may seem at the time. Eventually the husband will learn that if he insists on having sexual contact, he must get on with it without amorous embellishment.

As soon as the husband has completed the act, the wise wife will start nagging him about various minor tasks she wishes him to perform on the morrow. Many men obtain a major portion of their sexual satisfaction from the peaceful exhaustion immediately after the act is over. Thus the wife must insure that there is no peace in this period for him to enjoy. Otherwise, he might be encouraged to soon try for more.

One heartening factor for which the wife can be grateful is the fact that the husband's home, school, church, and social environment have been working together all through his life to instill in him a deep sense of guilt in regards to his sexual feelings, so that he comes to the marriage couch apologetically and filled with shame, already half cowed and subdued. The wise wife seizes upon this advantage and relentlessly pursues her goal first to limit, later to annihilate completely, her husband's desire for sexual expression.

After all the hectic preparations for the Big Day, many couples today opt for a few peaceful, relaxing weeks in sunny seclusion. But honeymoons haven't always been languorous and restful.

A month of wine and honey

THE EARLIEST HONEYMOONS were not necessarily periods of happy celebration for newlyweds, but rather forced seclusion for the bride. In the days when marriage by abduction was not yet outlawed, a groom would capture a bride from a village or rival tribe and take her into seclusion until tempers had cooled or the tribe had moved on. The groom would often return alone to negotiate a bride-price with her father to prevent an outbreak of fighting. The kidnapped bride would be held captive and sedated with honey wine for a full cycle of the moon, after which time the couple was considered married. Out of this tradition, eloping couples that ran off together and drank honey wine for a month, "until the moon waned," were considered married.

THE IRISH translation for honeymoon is *mi na meala*, which means the "month of honey." This stems from the ancient Germanic tribal custom of the newlyweds' drinking mead laced with honey—in preparation for the bitter and the sweet of marriage—every day for a full cycle of the moon. This month of honey became known as the honeymoon.

IN JAPAN, it was customary for the groom to prepare for the honeymoon by overseeing the installation of the bridal bed the day before the wedding. A "good luck woman" or a "good luck man"—that is, a man or woman with many children and a living mate was selected to "install" the newly purchased bed. After the bed was in place, children were invited onto the bed as an omen of fertility. The bed was scattered with red dates, oranges, lotus seeds, peanuts, pomengranates, and other fruits for the same reason.

Top 5 Honeymoon Locations

HAWAII With its perfect weather, volcanoes, valleys, waterfalls, nightlife, and black sand beaches, Hawaii is the ideal honeymoon destination for newlyweds.

WALT DISNEY WORLD Get ready to be a kid again. Any one of the great honeymoon packages offers deluxe accommodations at a select Disney resort and unlimited passes to any of the fun-filled theme parks.

ITALY Take a gondola ride in Venice. Bask in the Renaissance beauty of Florence. Rent a villa on Lake Como. No matter what your destination is, Italy will not disappoint.

NIAGARA FALLS A long-time traditional location for honeymoons. Newlyweds can ride a boat under the majestic falls in the Maid of the Mist.

PARIS, FRANCE It's not called the most romantic city for nothing! Stroll along the Seine, take in a museum, or have a romantic dinner at one of the hundreds of brasseries. Paris really is for lovers!

IN BULGARIA the bride and groom disappear for a week to spend their first days as husband and wife in seclusion. The bride then makes a visit to the village well, accompanied by a group of married women. She circles the well three times and kisses the hands of all of the women who have come with her. The women then present her with figs to wish her a fruitful and happy life.

When I first got engaged, all I did was stare at my new diamond ring. Ooooh, look how shiny it is. Ooooh, look how it sparkles. Doesn't it look nice as I'm typing on my keyboard; doesn't it look nice as I'm walking down the street; doesn't it look nice with everything I own; and wouldn't it look even nicer with a new handbag, skirt, or pair of Jimmy Choo shoes? This new diamond ring had become a symbol of the promise of a wholenew shiny life—marriage. But let's talk about the other defining characteristic of a diamond: the fact that it can cut through glass. Because as shiny and fabulous as marriage often is, it can also be hard as hell.

I DO. I DID. NOW WHAT?!

BY JENNY LEE

I was wholly unprepared for how big an impact marriage would have on my life. Sure I was into the whole "wedding" thing—all my friends in one room, the fabulous Vera Wang dress that makes me feel like a queen, and, of course, the cake. I mean, who doesn't like a good party where she's the guest of honor and everyone can't help but smile and fawn. I felt as if I'd won a beauty contest or something. But what I'm talking about is the aftermath, the stillness after the storm, when you peek out to see if your mailbox is still standing—after the room service of club sandwiches and French fries (I hadn't eaten in months); after the five-hundred-dollar silk negligee is lying on the floor, having made its all-too-brief appearance (I think I wore the damn thing for like three minutes tops); and after he's fallen asleep, when you find yourself in the dark thinking, I'm married. Now what?

It's just that no one clues you in ahead of time about everything that's involved. Sure, your mom has told you plenty, but over the years you've learned to dismiss her advice almost automatically— she's practically a Flintstone as far as you're concerned. Like you're really going to spend your weekends ironing and making casseroles. I certainly tried to get some inkling from my few married friends of what was to come after the "I do"s, but they'd just shrug, then emphatically pronounce that my wedding day would be one of the best days of my life. Next, their eyes starry, they would begin to tell me about their own wedding, speaking in a strange, hushed tone; I'd interrupt them and say, "Yes, I remember; I was there—it was certainly magical, and you looked really really thin—but c'mon, tell me about after the wedding. What's life like *after* the dress? What is it like to be a wife?"

I half imagined there might be some secret marriage pact that says you can't share the mysteries of marriage with the world of the single. But what's the big secret? The suspense kept me up nights for a while, but eventually I chalked it up to my not having had chocolate for weeks (in hopes of having skinny arms for my wedding photos).

I figured I just had a little prewedding paranoia, right? In fact, maybe the reason no one could tell me the real deal about marriage is because it's so utterly amazing they don't even know where to start. Now we're talking.

Well, what it came down to is that I had absolutely no clue what to expect from marriage. I'm not saying that was necessarily a bad thing, but I will say that I wish I had seen the sign that said BUCKLE UP, WILD RIDE AHEAD. The beginning of a marriage is a roller coaster of huge life changes, and we all know what that means—major emotional loop de loops.

So you get married, and you're incredibly happy. The honeymoon is a blast (in case you didn't know, honeymoon calories don't count!), and when you get back, you're still totally euphoric, even though you have to go back to work. You move in together (unless you're already shacked up), and then you wake up one morning, walk into the kitchen, and suddenly you're like, "What have I done? Why did I get married? WHO ON EARTH WOULD LEAVE A MUSTARD-COVERED KNIFE ON A CLEAN KITCHEN TOWEL, AND HOW COULD I BE LEGALLY BOUND TO SUCH A MAN?"

So fine, your emotions fluctuate a bit; we all deal with that every month. After a while you realize that a lot of things that seemed like very big deals at the time are not so big when you think of them relative to the next sixty years of your life. What's one kitchen towel in the grand scheme of things if you never again have to take out the trash? I mean, when you think about marriage and all that goes with it (the in-laws, the mortgage, your married friends, the fact that you can't ever get him to fill up the Brita water pitcher), it can seem terribly complicated. But at its very core it's almost laughably and profoundly simple. The four things that you need are love (because there will be a day when you catch him using your expensive shampoo), effort (walking to the video store is not considered a night out on the town), time (keep in mind that you'll never ever be able to do everything on your to-do list, so you might as well have some fun together because, trust me, the laundry will still be there tomorrow), and, most important (well, in *my* humble opinion) a sense of humor (if you look hard enough, you can find laughter in almost any situation).

In some ways marriage is everything I've ever wanted (someone to kill the spiders and change the lightbulbs). But it's not quite the glass-slipper fantasy—you know, where you marry the prince, live in a castle, throw fabulous parties, and buy shoes all the time. Married life contains an inordinate amount of everyday challenges with which you have to learn to deal, and the responsibilities are forever—till death do you part. But then…you can be surprised. One night when you're very cranky, and all the shows are repeats, and you've already read all the fashion mags for the month, and you're in the bedroom trying on your old party shoes thinking that your feet are all dressed up with no place to go—your husband, your prince, will suddenly appear by your side…and present you with a grilled cheese sandwich that he's made just for you.

BEAUTY AND THE BEAST

By Madame LePrince de Beaumont

In one of the first printed versions of this classic fairytale, author Madame LePrince de Beaumont tells the story of Beauty, a princess who falls in love with a kind and virtuous beast, despite his horrid appearance. In the following excerpt, Beauty declares her wish to marry the Beast and discovers that sometimes appearances can be very deceiving.

"…dear beast, you shall not die," said Beauty. "You will live in order to become my husband. From this moment on, I give you my hand and I swear that I shall be yours alone. Alas! I thought that I felt only friendship for you, but the sorrow that I feel now makes me see that I cannot live without you."

Hardly had Beauty spoken these words when she saw the castle blazing with lights—there were fireworks and music and everything to indicate a celebration. None of these wonders held her attention, however; she turned her eyes back toward her dear beast….But to her surprise, the beast had disappeared and at her feet she saw instead a prince handsomer than the god of love, who thanked her for having ended his enchantment. Although this prince deserved all her attention, she could not help asking where the beast was.

"You see him at your feet," the prince told her. "A wicked fairy had condemned me to remain in that shape until a beautiful girl should agree to marry me, and she had forbidden me to reveal my wit and intelligence.

You were the only person in the world good enough to let yourself be moved by the goodness of my character, and in offering you my crown, I am only freeing myself of my obligations to you."

Beauty, pleasantly surprised, gave her hand to this handsome prince to help him to rise. They went together to the castle, and Beauty almost died of joy to find in the great hall her father and all her family, transported to the castle by the beautiful lady who had appeared to her in a dream.

"Beauty," said the lady, who was a powerful fairy, "come and receive the reward of your good choice. You have preferred virtue to handsomeness and wit and you deserve to find all these qualities united in one single person. You are going to become a great queen...."

Saying this, the fairy waved her wand, and everyone who was in the hall was transported to the prince's kingdom. His subjects received him with joy, and he married Beauty, who lived with him for a long time in a state of happiness that was perfect because it was based upon virtue.

NEWLYWED DINNER

The wedding may be over, but your life as a married couple is just beginning. Keep the passion of your honeymoon alive with an aphrodisiac dinner for two to celebrate your first month (or week!) together. Throughout history, certain foods have been believed to stimulate the libido because of their suggestive shapes, texture, or nutritional content. Second-century Roman satirist Juvenal was the first to note the amorous nature of women after consuming large quantities of wine and "giant oysters," which not only resemble female genitalia, but are also very rich in protein. Another powerful sexual stimulant is chocolate, which the Aztecs relished as the "nourishment of the gods." In the towns of France, eating strawberries is still considered to be an extremely potent way for newlyweds to nourish their libido.

Create the mood for romance by setting a romantic candlelit table for two. Then stir up some passion with this aphrodisiac-laden menu:

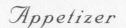

CHAMPAGNE OYSTERS WITH POTATO CAKES

POTATO CAKES

2 large potatoes, cleaned, peeled, and grated

½ large onion, finely chopped

1 tablespoon fresh lemon juice

1 large egg, lightly beaten

1 tablespoon chopped fresh parsley

Salt and freshly ground pepper to taste

2 tablespoons vegetable oil

1. Preheat the oven to 200° F. Place a baking sheet on middle rack of oven.

2. In a medium-sized bowl combine the grated potatoes and chopped onions. Add the lemon juice and toss.

3. Place the potato and onion mixture in a clean kitchen towel and squeeze dry. Transfer to a small bowl and add the egg and parsley. Mix well. Season with salt and pepper.

4. Using the palms of your hands, form mixture into 2 patties.

5. Heat vegetable oil in a large skillet, over medium heat. Add the potato cakes to the skillet, pressing down on each patty until flat and even all the way around. Sauté the potato cakes until golden brown (about 3 minutes for each side.)

6. Transfer to baking sheet in the oven to keep warm while you are preparing the oysters.

CHAMPAGNE OYSTERS

½ cup champagne

1 ½ tablespoons finely chopped shallots

¾ cup heavy cream

4 tablespoons unsalted butter, softened

12 oysters, freshly shucked

1 tablespoon fresh thyme

1 teaspoon chives

Salt and pepper to taste

1. In a medium saucepan, combine the champagne and shallots over medium heat. Simmer until the liquid is reduced by half.

2. Slowly add the cream, whisking constantly. Return to a simmer until liquid is reduced by one quarter. Slowly add the butter, a tablespoon at a time, whisking until thickened.

3. Add the oysters to the sauce and simmer gently until the oysters are firm. Add thyme, and season with salt and pepper.

4. To serve, place potato patties on prewarmed plates and spoon 6 oysters onto each cake. Drizzle sauce over the oysters, top with caviar (optional), and sprinkle with chives. Serve immediately.

Serves 2

Entrée
LOBSTER & LINGUINE WITH TOMATO-BASIL SAUCE

*2 small live lobsters
(1 to 1 ¼ lbs each)*

*1 tablespoon
extra-virgin olive oil*

*1 tablespoon
chopped garlic*

*3 cups chopped fresh
vine-ripened tomatoes
or 1 14-ounce can
tomatoes (with juices)*

¼ cup dry white wine

*½ cup slivered
basil leaves*

¼ cup light cream

*salt and freshly
ground black pepper*

1 lb. fresh linguine

1. In a large pot, bring 2 inches water to a boil. Put lobsters in headfirst, cover tightly and steam until the lobsters are bright red, 10 to 12 minutes. Remove and let cool slightly. Separate tails from bodies, twist off claws, remove all the meat and cut into large chunks; discard shells.

2. In a large deep skillet, heat oil over medium-high heat. Add garlic and sauté until the garlic is tender, about 2 minutes. Stir in tomatoes and wine and bring to a simmer. Add 1/4 cup of the basil and continue to simmer until the sauce has thickened slightly (about 2 minutes). Add salt and pepper to taste.

3. Remove the skillet from the heat, add cream and toss to combine. Add the reserved lobster meat to the sauce.

4. Meanwhile, cook linguine in a large pot of boiling salted water until al dente (2 to 3 minutes). Drain the linguine and toss with the sauce. Garnish with the remaining basil and serve.

Serves 2

CHOCOLATE-DIPPED STRAWBERRIES

½ pint fresh strawberries, stems intact

4 ounces bittersweet chocolate, broken into chunks

½ tablespoon solid white vegetable shortening

½ cup of white chocolate chips

1. Rinse strawberries thoroughly under running water, pat with paper towels, and leave to air-dry.

2. Pour about 1 inch of water into bottom of a double boiler and heat over low heat until hot but not simmering. Melt the milk chocolate and shortening together in the top of double boiler, stirring occasionally until smooth.

3. Working quickly, swirl each strawberry gently in the chocolate about halfway up the fruit and place on a piece of wax paper to cool and harden. When cool, place in refrigerator to further set chocolate shell, about a half hour.

4. Meanwhile, clean and replace the top of your double boiler, and use to melt white chocolate chips, stirring until smooth over low heat.

5. Place cooled strawberries on serving dish and drizzle with melted white chocolate. Refrigerate until you are ready to serve. They go perfectly with a chilled glass of champagne.

Serves 2 (with some left over for a midnight snack!)

A good marriage is that in which each

RAINER MARIA RILKE

appoints the other guardian of his solitude.

You and I
Have so much love,
That it
Burns like a fire,
In which we bake a lump of clay
Molded into a figure of you
And a figure of me.
Then we take both of them,
And break them into pieces,
And mix the pieces with water,
And mold again a figure of you,
And a figure of me.
I am in your clay.
You are in my clay.
In life we share a single quilt.
In death we will share one bed.

MARRIED LOVE
Kuan Tao-Sheng

Marriage is one long conversation, chequered by disputes... But in the intervals, almost unconsciously, and with no desire to shine, the whole material of life is turned over and over ideas are struck out and shared, the two persons more and more adapt their notions one to suit the other, and in process of time, without sound of trumpet, they conduct each other into new worlds of thought.

ROBERT LOUIS STEVENSON (1850–1894)

My parents have been married for over forty years. I cannot judge whether it has been a satisfying marriage, but it has endured through moments of crisis and great pain and so, on some level, it has been a success. In trying to come to terms with my own marriage, I find myself looking back.

LOOKING BACK
FROM FROM THE HEART

From my own observations (and without the benefit of statistically significant sampling or scientific inquiry), it seems that marriages of long duration have rituals that form the fabric of the relationship. As in my parents' case, arguing is an important one.

I often think about the scene repeated year after year in my home during the Jewish holidays. On each holiday my mother and grandmother would spend a frenzied day completing the preparations for the evening meal— cooking and baking, seasoning and tasting, and seasoning yet again. Each holiday morning, as my father left for work, my mother would admonish him to come home early. That evening my father would invariably return and hour late, wilted flowers in hand, muttering about the terrible holiday traffic (which he seemed to regard as a completely unexpected development even though holiday traffic was very bad every year).

My mother, of course, would be waiting at the door and, upon my father's arrival, burst into a litany of angry complaints about the ruined meal—how she had worked all day to prepare a wonderful dinner and now the pot roast was overcooked and the vegetables were limp and, worst of all, the family would have to rush through the meal so my father could get to synagogue on time. He would invariably throw up his hands and, in turn, complain about how hard he worked and how my mother always gave him a hard time regardless of what he did. A few minutes later we would sit down to dinner all the while assuring my mother that the food tasted just fine.

After watching this scene year after year, I finally asked why she just did not prepare a simpler meal or start cooking later in the day, since she knew my father always came home late on the holidays. (And on every other occasion, since my father, as optimistic about travel times as he is about every other aspect of his life, always assumed there would be clear roads and strong tailwinds.) She rebuked me for interfering in an area that was none of my concern and then pointedly informed me that she and my father enjoyed having this argument.

At the time I was puzzled by her response. After all, it did not look like they were enjoying themselves. Now, after more than a decade of being married, I think I understand. The Jewish holiday fight was a safety valve for them, an opportunity to vent their frustrations safely. Since it was, after all, a holiday, they had to make up quickly. Moreover, it had become a ritual for them and gave them a sense of continuity and comfort.

In my own marriage, our arguments have essentially the same theme, which, come to think of it is not so different from my parents'. Wife to husband: "If you really loved me, you would be more sensitive to my needs (that is, share more of the household burden, give me more emotional support, value what is important to me)." Husband to wife: "If you really loved me, you would appreciate me for who I am, stop expecting me to change, and stop nagging me."

With a high degree of accuracy I can predict we will have this fight (in one variation or another) not on the Jewish holidays but on the first day of any vacation, on Mother's Day (the unnatural reversal of roles creates tension in our house), and before we go out (my husband puts on his oldest clothes, I express outrage, he tells me I am a nag and then changes into something acceptable, something he probably intended to wear all along).

Not only do our arguments have the same theme, but like many other couples, I suspect, our arguments have certain parameters. Fighting is unacceptable in front of certain people—professional associates, in-laws, acquaintances, and even certain friends—and is certainly restrained (but, for better or worse, not avoided) in front of the children.

More important, although we have never acknowledged this to each other, there are certain things we will never say, even in the heat of battle, because we know instinctively that, once said, these words can never be forgiven. The forbidden words relate to those areas the other person is most acutely and painfully sensitive about, the words that, daggerlike, quickly and sharply pierce the heart.

Reflecting on the highly structured, repetitive nature of our arguments, it seems that they actually strengthen our marriage, rather than weaken it. We can let off steam within accepted boundaries, in ways we know will not "rend us asunder." We can secretly mouth the other's expected rejoinders when we begin to argue, and we know when it is time to stop.

In the end, I suppose, what makes a marriage last is not how much you love the other person but how the marriage provides structure, comfort, and predictability in a world that is chaotic, uncontrollable, and profoundly indifferent.

Elizabeth

Never go to bed angry.
Stay up and fight.
PHYLLIS DILLER

ADVICE: *Don't Go to Bed Mad*

I learned this bit of wisdom from my parents, and I've appreciated it my entire life. When you have an absolute policy that no one goes to bed mad, it helps you remember that love and forgiveness are never far away. It encourages you to bend a little, to be the first to reach out and open the dialogue, offer a genuine hug, and keep your heart open.

Kris and I have tried very hard to implement this strategy in our family. While it's not perfect, and while occasionally one or more of us seems a little frustrated at bedtime, on balance it's been enormously helpful. It ensures that ninety-nine times out of one hundred, we'll wake up the next morning with love in our hearts and with an attitude of "This is a new day." I hope that you'll give this strategy a fair try. It's certainly not always easy, and you probably won't bat 100 percent, but it's well worth the effort. Remember, life is short. Nothing is so important that its' worth ruining your day, nor is anything so significant that its' worth going to bed mad. Have a nice sleep.

—From *Don't Sweat the Small Stuff*, by Richard Carlson PHD.

*I*t's never too soon to start looking ahead! Every year, when the calendar falls on the anniversary of their wedding, married couples rekindle the romance and memories of their most important day.

Grow old along with me, the best is yet to be

Husbands and wives often spend their first anniversary alone together, while later anniversaries tend to be big celebratory bashes. In England, couples enjoying their diamond anniversary receive a special telegram from the queen. The custom of saving the top layer of the wedding cake to share on the first anniversary predates the icebox. In those days, cakes were made of dried fruit, alcohol, and marzipan, and could easily keep for a year or longer.

Anniversary Gifts

	TRADITIONAL	CONTEMPORARY
YEAR 1:	PAPER	CLOCKS
YEAR 2:	COTTON	CHINA
YEAR 3:	LEATHER	CRYSTAL, GLASS
YEAR 4:	LINEN	ELECTRICAL APPLIANCES
YEAR 5:	WOOD	SILVERWARE
YEAR 6:	IRON	WOOD
YEAR 7:	WOOL, COPPER, BRASS	DESK SETS
YEAR 8:	BRONZE	LINEN, LACE
YEAR 9:	POTTERY, WILLOW	LEATHER
YEAR 10:	TIN, ALUMINUM	DIAMOND JEWELRY
YEAR 11:	STEEL	FASHION JEWELRY
YEAR 12:	SILK	PEARLS
YEAR 13:	LACE	TEXTILES, FUR
YEAR 14:	IVORY	GOLD JEWELRY
YEAR 15:	CRYSTAL	WATCHES
YEAR 20:	CHINA	PLATINUM
YEAR 25:	SILVER	STERLING SILVER
YEAR 30:	PEARLS	DIAMONDS
YEAR 35:	CORAL	JADE
YEAR 40:	RUBIES	GARNETS
YEAR 45:	SAPPHIRES	TOURMALINES
YEAR 50:	GOLD	GOLD

Each night for the last week, as I have gone out to walk the dogs or leave the trash at the curb, the boy and girl have been shadows in the doorway of the house next door. Even when it was raining, lightning bisecting the sky, they were there, entangled in one of those kisses that last forever, that end only when the oxygen supply gives out. One night the boy spoke as the dogs sniffed at the steps below. "Do you know how much I love this girl?" he asked, a rhetorical boast to a middle-aged stranger.

"Oh, God," I said, tugging on the leashes, and though the lovers might have thought my response indicated disapproval, it was really the shock of recognition,

MARRIED
BY ANNA QUINDLEN

sharp and silver as the lightning. I remember being in love like this. Entering into a state more like a tropical disease than a relationship, listening to one catchy piece of bubble-gum music over and over again and getting the same odd feeling in the stomach and the chest. When I was in high school, the song was by the Beach Boys, "Wouldn't It Be Nice": "Though it's gonna make it that much better/When we can say goodnight and stay together." The big payoff. Not so much sex, at least for the girls, as a kind of mythical domesticity: napkins and matching place mats, unlimited kissing, no adults, flowers every day. What our parents referred to as playing house.

It's getting on to ten years that I've been married. I'm not sure when I realized that reality was going to be both something less and something much more. Luckily many of us know this before we marry, or there would be even more disasters than we now suffer through, many more people packing away an expensive wedding album in some corner of the basement where, it is hoped, it will mildew.

When I was younger, I tended to fall in love with just one thing: a kind of bravado, a certain smile. (The girl in the doorway, I am convinced, has fallen for blond hair and a crooked grin.) I even fell in love with a certain set of bony shoulders in a sport jacket years ago. But unlike a lot of my friends, who went through more than a few Mr. Wrongs and have now settled down with Mr. Maybe, I married the person inside the sport jacket. And I held on like a dog with a bone to a love affair between a girl whose idea of awesome responsibility was a psych midterm and a boy who painted his dorm room black, long after that boy and girl were gone. I held onto what has been going on in that doorway long past the time when I was really too old to believe in magic.

Truth is, I still believe in magic, and it's still there, although there's no point denying that it is occasionally submerged beneath a welter of cereal bowls, dirty shirts, late nights, early mornings, and all the other everyday things that bubble-gum music never reflects. But what I didn't know about marriage, the less magical parts of it, has become perhaps more important to me. Now we have history as well as chemistry. An enormous part of my past does not exist without my husband. An enormous part of my present, too. I still feel somehow that things do not really happen to me unless I have told them to him. I don't mean this nonsense about being best friends, which I have never been able to cotton to; our relationship is too judgmental, too demanding, too prickly to have much in common with the quiet waters of friendship. Like emotional acupuncturists, we know just where to put the needle. And do.

But we are each other's family. And while I know people who have cut their families loose, who think them insignificant or too troublesome to be part of their lives, I am not one of those people. I came late to the discovery that we would be related by marriage. I once made a fool of myself in front of a friend in the emergency room of a small resort hospital after my husband's stomach and a bad fried clam had had an unfortunate meeting. "Are either of you related to him?" the nurse asked, and we both shook our heads until our friend prodded me gently in the side. "Oh, well, I'm his wife," I said.

There is something so settled and stodgy about turning a great romance into next of kin on an emergency room form, and something so soothing and special, too. I suppose that is what I find so dreadful about divorce; lovers are supposed to leave you in the lurch, but your family is supposed to stick by you forever. "You can pick your friends, but you can't pick your relations," the folksy folks always say. Ah, but in this one case you can. You just don't realize it at the time.

What does it mean that I do not envy the two of them, standing in the doorway, locked together like Romeo and Juliet in the tomb? I suppose when I was their age I would have assumed it meant that I was old and desiccated. But of course what has really happened is that I know the difference now between dedication and infatuation.

That doesn't mean I don't still get an enormous kick out of infatuation: the exciting ephemera, the punch in the stomach, the adrenaline to the heart. At a cocktail party the other night I looked across a crowded room and was taken by a stranger, in half profile, a handsome, terribly young-looking man with a halo of backlighted curls. And then he turned and I realized that it was the stranger I am married to, the beneficiary on my insurance policy, the sport jacket, the love of my life.

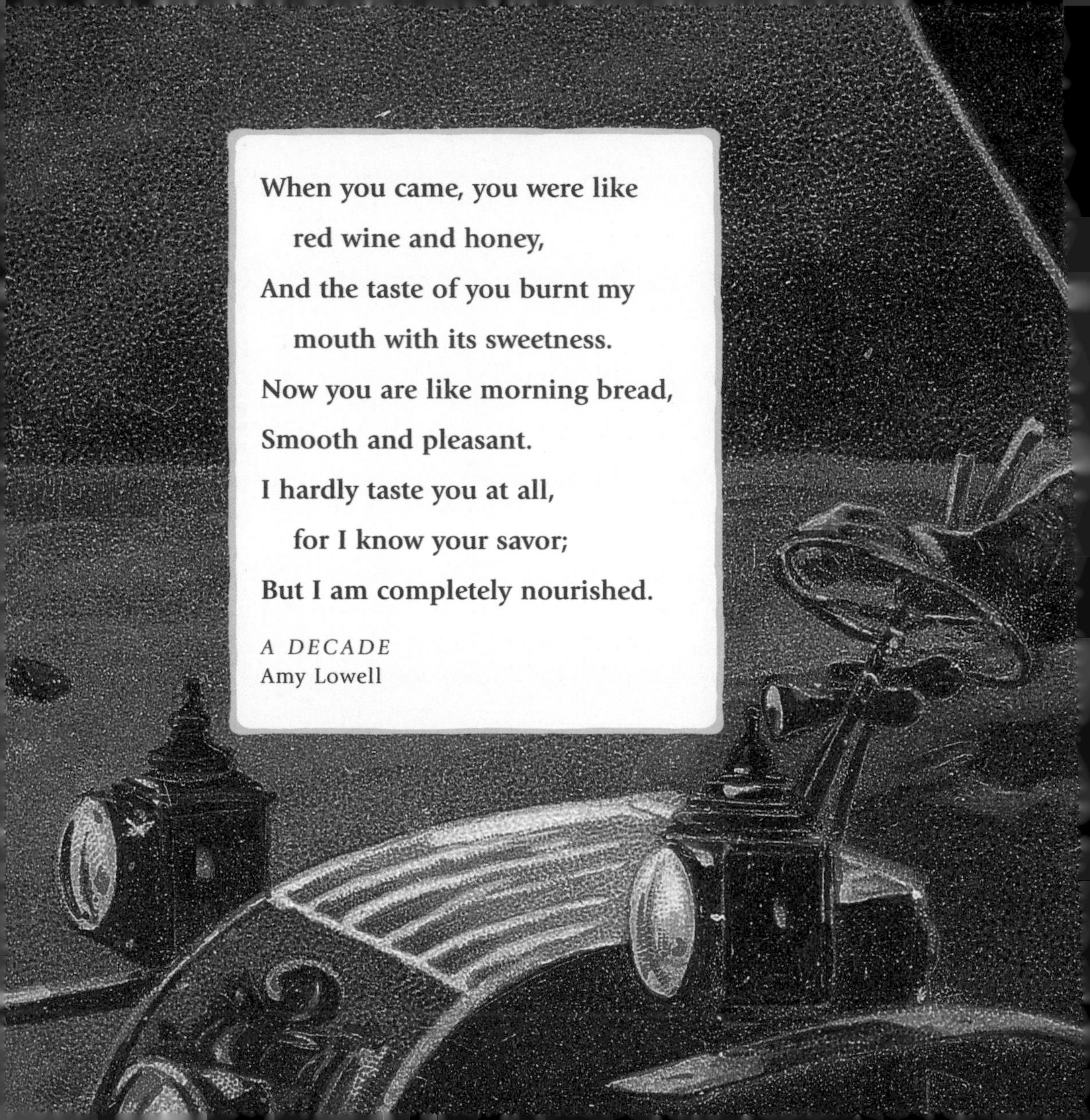

When you came, you were like
   red wine and honey,
And the taste of you burnt my
   mouth with its sweetness.
Now you are like morning bread,
Smooth and pleasant.
I hardly taste you at all,
   for I know your savor;
But I am completely nourished.

A DECADE
Amy Lowell

CORELLI'S MANDOLIN

BY LOUIS DE BERNIÈRES

Corelli's Mandolin is an epic tale about the enduring hope of love and the cruelty of war, set on a Greek island during World War II. When a young fisherman leaves to fight in the Greek army, his girlfriend falls for an officer in the occupying Italian army. As she struggles between conflicting feelings of loyalty and love, she receives some wise counsel from her father.

AND ANOTHER THING. Love is a temporary madness, it erupts like volcanoes and then subsides. And when it subsides you have to make a decision. You have to work out whether your roots have so entwined together that it is inconceivable that you should ever part. Because this is what love is. Love is not breathlessness, it is not excitement, it is not the promulgation of promises of eternal passion....That is just being "in love," which any fool can do. Love itself is what is left over when being in love has burned away, and this is both an art and a fortunate accident. Your mother and I had it, we had roots that grew towards each other underground, and when all the pretty blossom had fallen from our branches we found that we were one tree and not two.

SOWING THE SEEDS OF LOVE

THE CUSTOM OF PLANTING a flower bush or tree as a symbol of stability, growth, and fertility has long played a part in marriages and weddings. In many places around the world, newlyweds still celebrate their union with this ritual. In the village of Lucerne, Switzerland, couples plant pine trees to promote happiness and fertility. This dates back to an ancient tradition in which the groom proposed to his beloved by planting trees in her yard embellished with large decorative ribbons. In Holland, the houses of the newly married can be distinguished by the presence of freshly turned soil and newly planted lilies-of-the-valley. It is thought that these flowers represent a "return of happiness" that is renewed with their blooming every spring. The following planting instructions are for the bridal wreath spirea, a popular, beautiful, and aptly named shrub to use for this romantic tradition.

PLANTING A BRIDAL WREATH

❧ The bridal wreath spirea is one of the least finicky flowering shrubs out there, and can prove to be quite hardy. Before planting the bridal bush, clear a spot in the garden of any sod or weeds. Make sure that it is an open space with lots of sunlight—bridal wreaths grow very quickly, and after many years can reach a maximum width of 20 feet and a height of 6 to 10 feet.

❧ It is a good idea to keep the roots together with the soil they came in. Never let the roots come in contact with fresh manure or any other kind of fertilizer.

❧ Spread the roots evenly around in the hole, and make sure that the soil is packed carefully to cover the roots without any air pockets.

❧ To prevent too much water drainage, pack the soil around the top so that it forms a dish around the bush.

❧ Once the soil has been packed, give the bush a heavy watering. Don't worry about giving it too much water. Afterward, place a layer of mulch around the bush. Rotted bark, sawdust, or leaf mold will all help keep the soil moist.

❧ Be generous with water during the first season, but not to the point where the soil becomes soggy.

We take our usual walk this morning, although when I wake up I don't want to move. The dry desert winds stir up my allergies and I feel listless, out of sorts. Staring at my red-rimmed eyes and dry, grooved face as I brush my teeth doesn't help the mood. My hair, standing on end, refuses to be brushed into obedience.

Worse, my knees hurt. I feel like the Tin Woodman in *The Wizard of Oz*, who needed a shot of lubricating oil to get going. The connection of knees—father in wheelchair flashes unhappily in my mind. This was how he lost his independence. He couldn't rely on his knees to walk or drive safely.

OUR USUAL WALK
—from FROM THE HEART

"I'm not my father," I say to myself firmly. And more softly, tears just back of my eyes, "Oh, how I miss you, Dad."

"Let's go darling!" my husband's bright, cheery voice booms from the other room. He speaks loudly, to be heard over the morning news program. I want to go back to bed in silence.

Pete never takes silence for an answer. Knowing me well, he appears in the bedroom doorway to see if I'm dressed and over my rebellion. He resembles an overgrown boy in his turquoise whale sweatshirt (how could I ever have bought it?), bright red pants, mismatched socks, and run-down running shoes. "You'll feel much better once you get going," he says and kisses me.

His kisses always work magic, even when they're illogically timed.

"Okay," I mumble, giving in quickly, knowing he's right.

At our front door we turn left into the ocean breeze, lured by a view of the sea at the end of the street. We pass some teenagers hurrying to get to school in time for their first classes. Pete stops suddenly, grabs my hands, and kisses me. We both giggle. I imagine that any student who sees us thinks we're absurd—two antique creatures in baggy sweats in an embrace.

I feel lucky and blessed and embarrassed, all at once, ready to walk the earth with this man who rarely fails to delight me. Ready to do anything not to have my body go out on me, like the old woman we saw yesterday, frail and dried as an old leaf, clinging to a building for support, stopping for rest before she went on. He's right. I need the exercise to get my mental and physical kinks out.

We walk to the park bordering the beach, lost in our own thoughts. "See you at Willow Street," he says and begins to jog slowly, still-muscular legs as sturdy as ever, belly an unwelcome, perhaps permanent, visitor.

All the things I wanted to change in him now seem curiously appealing—his passion for golf, his sloppy habits, and his invariable optimism. Golf gives him exercise, friendship, and fresh air and helps him slug back at business frustration, and I'd rather pick up after him than have him be a nitpicker, railing at me for being sporadically messy. I know he'll never change. I don't want him to anymore. We are what we are, and somehow my occasional pessimism and his optimism are the perfect dancers, bridging the changing rhythms of life. And he's more thoughtful than ever, in all the important ways.

Where did all the years go? Gone, leaving us photographs on the family wall and a residue of the silver stardust that is love.

We meet again at Willow, our favorite street. "Do you still want a home here?" he asks, as though we aren't backed to the wall financially, as though we aren't in debt, as though the recession never happened.

"No," I answer, as if the choice is real. "I don't want a house anymore. I feel more secure in our condo because I'm not afraid to be alone when you're out of town. It's just right for the two of us."

"We could get a dog again," he smiles. "A big Saint Bernard, just like Reggie." I think of the rainy night in 1979, when I could no longer deny that our marriage was in deep trouble. We were lying on the den floor in our tract home, Reggie happily curled between us. He petted the dog languidly, never thinking of reaching out for me. I remember the ache of being unwanted, of getting up silently and going to bed without washing my face, pretending I was asleep when he came in. When I'm upset, I don't pretend anymore. I talk about it. I don't have the patience to wait. I've learned that much. The more honest I am, the less seems to come up.

The street slopes imperceptibly uphill, but my lungs want more air than I can take in and I fall behind his brisk pace. He turns missing me.

"I'm not too speedy this morning," I pant. "Go ahead. I'll catch up."

"No. I don't ever want to leave you behind," he says and slows to take my hand and kiss me tenderly.

We're here for each other in a way we never were before, when we glossed over our differences to preserve the image of the perfect marriage. Here we are, wrinkles, bellies, and all, laughing more than ever at the foibles we no longer try to change.

I reach up like a young bride to touch his face, the curve of his cheek, and tilt my face to kiss him. I think I'd rather be here, right now, right this moment, feeling this way, than be young again with perfect knees. I laugh at the unspoken joy that bubbles up, and he looks at me and says appreciatively, "Does any couple laugh as much as we do?" He slides his right hand under the band of my sweatpants, grabbing my behind, knowing I never wear underpants on our walks for exactly this moment.

"No couple I know," I respond. "My behind is getting so much smaller!" We both laugh again at my forty-year battle with a flabby butt.

"I can hardly find it," he says, so sincere I almost believe him.

We walk on, little slower now. His thoughts, I can tell, are on business. Mine linger on children, grandchildren, and marriage.

So it has come to this: Noticing thoughts fly through my mind like a flock of birds. I choose this one and that, not feeling their prisoner—most of the time. Noticing we're in the fall of our lives, amazed that spring and summer have gone…wondering when winter will come.

Charlotte

Understand, I'll slip quietly

away from the noisy crowd

when I see the pale

stars rising, blooming, over the oaks.

I'll pursue solitary pathways

through the pale twilit meadows,

with only this one dream:

You come too.

Rainer Maria Rilke

THE ADVENTURES OF SALLY

BY P. G. WODEHOUSE

Set in New York City in the 1920s, The Adventures of Sally *is the humorous story of a charming, headstrong young woman entering adulthood. In this excerpt, Sally receives some advice about men and marriage from her brother's fiancé, Gladys.*

"He is a chump, you know. That's what I love about him. That and the way his ears wiggle when he gets excited. Chumps always make the best husbands. When you marry, Sally, grab a chump. Tap his forehead first, and if it rings solid, don't hesitate. All the unhappy marriages come from the husband having brains. What good are brains to a man? They only unsettle him."

Published in 2003 by Welcome Books
An imprint of Welcome Enterprises, Inc.
6 West 18th Street, New York, NY, 10011
(212) 989-3200; Fax (212) 989-3205
email: info@welcomebooks.biz
www.welcomebooks.biz

Publisher: Lena Tabori
Project Director: Katrina Fried
Designer: Jon Glick
Assistant Project Director: Jacinta O'Halloran
Traditions & Lore: Monique Peterson
Recipes and Activities: Monique Peterson, Katrina Fried, and
Jacinta O'Halloran
Project Assistants: Amy Bradley, Nicholas Liu, Jasmine
Faustino, and Marta Sparago
Production Assistants: Naomi Irie and Kathryn Shaw
Activities line illustrations by Lawrence Chesler, Kathryn Shaw,
and Amy Bradley

Distributed to the trade in the U.S. and Canada by
Andrews McMeel Distribution Services
Order Department and Customer Service: (800) 223-2336
Orders Only Fax: (800) 943-9831

Library of Congress Cataloging-in-Publication Data on file.

Printed in Singapore
First Edition
10 9 8 7 6 5 4 3 2 1

I married beneath me.
All women do.

LADY NANCY ASTOR (1897–1964),
BRITISH POLITICIAN